ROME TOR

Wear the Fox Hat

Ecallaw Leachim

ROME TOR
Wear the Fox Hat

Author: Ecallaw Leachim

Being the continuing Saga of the Delphic Oracle and
Eruptus Non-Funnius, her troupe of Un-Funny Comedians,
as they save the world from certain destruction by
solving the problem of Ancient Dragons, bad tempered
blacksmiths, and too much imagination.

Ladder to
the Moon
Publications

Truth and fact are old-fashioned and out-of-date, my friends,
fit only for the dull and vulgar to live by. Appearance, not
reality, is what the clever dog grasps at in these clever days.
We spurn the dull-brown solid earth; we build our lives and
homes in the fair-seeming rainbow-land of shadow and chimera.

Jerome K Jerome

INDEX

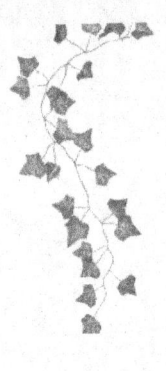

Rome TOR

COPYRIGHT 2022 Ladder to the Moon
This book is published under the Berne Convention. All
copyright protected to the author. No prior use
without permission except for excerpts for review or
educational purposes. All enquiries via Email to:
    info.numberharmonics@gmail.com
Published by Ladder to the Moon Publications.
ISBN 978-0-6452723-2-1

Other Books by this Author:

Psychic Nazi Hunter
(The Extraordinary Biography of Alan Wood-Thomas)

End of Times Trilogy (Sci Fi)
Eat Your Fill - Eat Your Religion - Eat Your God

The Book of Number Trilogy   (Mantic Science)
Workbook - Interpretations - Practitioner Guide

Jermimiah Versus the Grabblesnatch (Fiction - Myth)

The Divinity Dice Series (Mantic Science)
Decimal Dice - Divinity Dice - Book of Aspects - Pythagorean Patterns

Ratology: Way of the Un-Dammed (Non-Fiction)

Ratology II: Who Gives a Rats? (Non-Fiction)

Fragments of the Mirror (Short Stories)

Witch Hunter and other stories (Short Stories)

Water: More Precious than Gold (Non-Fiction)

The Borringbar War (3 Day Auto Biography)

Hello Planet Earth (Short Stories - Modern Myth)

Rome Too / Rome Tree (Parody)

Parables of Geoff (Biography)

The Wand (Fantasy)

Wolves of Planet Hope (Sci Fi)

Planet Aqua (Sci Fi)

Book of Yeshua (Historical Fiction)

Ladder to
the Moon
Publications

Available on Amazon or at
www.laddertothemoon.com.au

Conversation on the Rowing Bench

"Hey Neighbor - how would you rate your experience of the rowing bench?"

"It sucks, of course. What you want?"

"The travel part of this gig is good but the food is not much. I am running a survey to see what people want on the menu, and because it is pasta I am asking people if they prefer Spaghetti or Fettuccini?"

"Man, I love Spaghetti, who doesn't?"

"My other neighbor, he says no."

"He prefers Fettuccini?"

"Neither - He is crazy, doesn't like Pasta at all, he reckons."

"Well, has he had it with Garlic Bread?"

"I will ask."

(muttering sound)

"Says he doesn't like garlic."

"What, is he a vampire?"

"I will ask."

(muttering sound)

"No, says he isn't a vampire."

"Man, be careful. This is EXACTLY what a vampire would say!"

Return to Delphi

The rich and privileged never understand that, away from dinner parties where nostrils are filled with caviar stuffed repugnancy, there are places you are graced with the more down-to-earth odors. Some might say smells, the unkind would say stench. This latter most definitely applies when you sit on the slave bench of a Roman Trireme, for it is a fact of life that when you are chained to the oars the notion of getting up and going to the toot is not regarded favorably by the invariably bald, bad tempered, and sweaty slave master who is walking around with a whip.

Ergo, the galley of the slave ships tended to be somewhat ripe. However, not everyone there was a slave, for some paid for their passage with a little effort at the oars. These Souls lived above the status of a slave and were not chained into place. They could get up and get some fresh air and in an ideal world, this was so. The problem was that slave masters tend to be rather stupid and do not exactly keep a list in their mind of who is and isn't a slave, so you are likely to get a precautionary whip across the back before he remembers.

And you can't put your hand up to ask a question, because you will most certainly get a whip for taking your hands off the oars, so you are better doing a runner and hoping he will miss.

This will cause him to lunge in order to strike you. When he grasps you are not a slave, he may well apologize - Or he may get upset that you forced him into the extra effort, and beat you again to remind you of this. The morale is, it is far better to be rich and thus able to afford a passage, which was indeed the case with the now fabulously wealthy and popular troupe of unfunny comedians, Eruptus Non-Funnius.

Above the stirring oars, calmly contemplating life, sat the Delphic Oracle. The gentle breeze, the slapping of the waves, the deep blue of the ocean - all spoke of how they were nearing Greece once more. She sighed, it had been so wonderful escaping to New Rome, but now it was back to work - time to return to the sanctuary. As the ragged cliffs and striking coast line of Old Greece hove to in the distance, she went down to her cabin to dress for the journey.

Rufus, who was NOT rowing for once, was sitting in the shade eating grapes while ignoring Ofal, whose main occupation at that point was not bringing up his breakfast, and who had chosen to become a part-time rower to distract himself from seasickness.

As his fellow unfunny comedian and traveling companion sat there hauling away on the oars, he called up to Rufus, discussing the wisdom of keeping yourself occupied. "At least when you are rowing you keep your mind on what you are doing, not on how everything is moving," Ofal said wisely, or at least he thought this was wisdom.

Rufus continued with his earnest attempt at pretending Ofal wasn't there. His initial response to the comment was to wonder exactly what sort of mind Ofal had, or even if he had one, and was about to make an observation on his friends general state of stupid when he stopped himself. That was the OLD Rufus. Now he was rich he had reformed. NOW he just *thought* wicked and sarcastic notions rather than speaking them and was currently learning to cast aspersions with an askance glance with the eyes rather than the acerbic slice with the tongue.

This small restraint was put in place by his solicitor who informed him how offending people was now going to cost him money. His initial response had been, "Slander is not slander if it is true!" To which his solicitor had responded, "Slender is not slender if it is fat."

"That doesn't make sense!" Rufus had protested.

In response, his friend and solicitor, the also now very rich Chincino, advised, "And if you keep your mouth shut instead of opening it you won't have to hire me to prove it."

Despite this minor inconvenience of keeping ones mouth shut, being rich was a delight. And after accepting that silence was indeed golden, because it saved you gold, Rufus relaxed into the lifestyle of the wealthy. For one, he was enjoying the fact he was eating grapes and not rowing. The possession of money meant you not only did not have to row for a fare, you could gaze out indolently onto the waters of the Atlantic while you fished, ate fruit and cheese, and generally lolled about - A pleasure spoiled only by travel companions who didn't have the decency to stop chundering into a bucket.

Which was why Ofal was back on the slave bench, to stop him looking at the vast ocean that was making him violently seasick. It did not stop him whining and complaining, however.

"I don't know why we are here, anyway," Ofal complained. "After all, it was just a message, could have been anyone. And what does *'the egg has gone missing!'* actually mean? Could have been a hoax. We might be suffering all this for nothing." he moaned.

Rufus diligently continued to pretend he heard nothing and looked over at the cheese board wondering what sort of a suffering it would be to have the Brie instead of the Camembert.

"By the Gods, I don't know how you can eat. Just the thought of food makes me nauseous." Ofal kept barreling along the misery highway, making sure everyone knew what a sad sack he was.

Making a choice as his response, Rufus picked the smelliest, ripest bit of gorgonzola he could find, and went down the stairs, right up to Ofal's nose, then bit into it, going, "Mmmmmm!" This pushed the seasick Ofal onto yet another round of convulsions, which put a small, satisfied smile on the face of Rufus. Finally, he noted, "Almost there old boy, you will soon be able to eat goat cheese (Ofal winced) and baklava (he double winced) and mounds of pasta!"

Ofal responded with a deep "Bleeeeeaaah" into his bucket.

At this point Meridius appeared from her cabin, dressed in her trekking gear. "We must go directly to Kirra," she said, to which Rufus paled. That was work, he wanted more luxury.

"But I thought our first stop would be Corinth! You know - night life, bars - a good time. Kirra is a fishing village with only one thing in its favor, the road that takes you away from it."

"Mmmm," said Meridius in her non-committal *'I am not listening to anything you say'* voice. "We need to get to Delphi, ASAP."

And that was it, she went back into her cabin. Rufus sighed, then went to give the message to the Captain. It had been well over a year since he had left the old country, traveling to New Rome with Meridius in tow. They had no idea she was the Oracle back then, but since that time they had ended animal sacrifice, convinced the medical community to use Chincino's miracle herb, aspirin, and to stop using leeches and blood-letting, while at the same time their small trio of Un-Funny Comedians had become quite famous - a household name and very wealthy.

Eruptus Non-Funnius were THE in-demand act at the best of Coliseums now. Coming back to Greece like this only meant a whole lot of shows they were not playing and buckets of cash not being carried to the wagon. Yes, she was the divine oracle, and yes, he had a lot to thank Meridius for, but honestly, the old country? And all because of a single message from an unconfirmed source?

The fact she was on first name terms with the Gods, you 'might' have thought she would have asked Zeus for a lift. He was there in New Rome, drinking their old friend Garam's cellar dry when they took the donkey cart to the wharves. The old bugger just waved goodbye as they left, snorting some white powder that the African Prince had brought back from Mexicanus.

"More of the special aspirin, Zeus?" Baraka Alashad had asked him as they went out the door.

This whole business of having to get back to Delphi was extremely inconvenient and almost certainly a waste of time. However, the reality was if they performed without Meridius, the only applause they would get would be people cheering them on as they carried their crucifixes up the hill. She was insanely popular.

Lose weight, see the world, experience foreign cultures and all for FREE! That was what the advertisement said. So many gullible fools fell for it.

Ox Cart to Delphi

Meridius sat serenely in the back of the cart as it bobbed slowly along the back roads of Greece. They had made landfall at Kirra, at the foot hills of Delphi, and quickly requested a donkey cart to take them up to the sanctuary. They barely spent ten minutes shifting their stage show into the back before they were gone, with Ofal immensely grateful for the lack of water underneath them.

Rufus spoke passable Greek, so while the Oracle dreamed away in the back of the cart he pulled up by a roadside stall in a small village and ordered some coffee and baklava to help get them over the journey. "Thank goodness we are rich enough to not have to row anymore," he said to Ofal who was helping him carry their takeaway back to the cart. "I tell you, the luxury of sails and ocean going barges, who would have ever dreamed we could have afforded such luxury?"

Ignoring the fact that he had rowed most of the way from New Rome to stave off the sea sickness, Ofal appeared concerned by a new sort of threat. "Why is everyone staring at us?"

"Hillbillies," snorted Rufus. "They never get to see anything in this backwater. I have no idea why Meridius insisted on landing here and rushing up to Delphi."

"It's because it is so close to Delhi!" Ofal explained as if this was news.

"And not very far from Corinth, which is a much better place to unload. Which brings up the question, why are we here with Meridius anyway? As soon as we arrive she will be whisked off and will be required to Oracle away for days and weeks. She has been gone for ages and I can but imagine the sort of backlog she will have to clear."

At this point, the locals tweaked as to who was in the back of the cart, and seemed to turn into zombies, staggering forward with their upraised arms, chanting, "Oracle - Oracle"

Meridius woke up and seemed to think this was perfectly normal. She popped upright to say hello, "Hello!" but the zombies zombied on - At which point she called out to Rufus, "Darlings, normally the men around me are supposed to get large sticks and beat the peasants off. The poor dears can't help themselves because I have been away so long. I know you love your coffee and sweets, but I don't suppose you both could be complete hugabugs and forget them so we can just leave?"

But then something caught her eye. She looked closer and held up her hand, which seemed to stop the march of zombies. "Darlings," she said, talking to the peasants, which seemed a very poor way to describe them. "Could one of you possibly explain why all you are wearing bits of FOX over your rags, is it the new fashion?"

At that point, the zombies ceased shambling forwards and looked very confused. Despite being rather stunned that the Oracle would speak to them, one of the peasants stammered out a response, "The Ogoglio!" he exclaimed, by apparent way of explanation.

Then, passably strange though it was, ALL of them start chanting "OGOGLIO! OGOGLIO!"

Rufus was in the process of assuming they had walked into some weird cult full of mindless creatures when it dawned on him, they were peasants, therefore most decidedly a weird cult of mindless creatures. To his surprise, however, Meridius smiled, saying, "Oh, good." It was as if the nonsense word meant something to her.

"And this Ogoglio word means?" Rufus asked.

"Mmmm," she answers as if that were an answer.

Then, addressing the crowd, "But why the bits of fox all over you?" she asked them.

A brave lad, trembling as he stepped forward, bowed and explained, "Dearest Oracle, it is because we cannot afford hats!"

If she was surprised by the new fashion of not affording hats, no one would know. Meridius didn't say much about it. Instead, she indicated for them all to line up, and, one by one, she spoke to their nervous and insecure selves, thanking them for looking after the village, the fishing boats, or whatever it was that they did. The people seemed happy that she was speaking to their miserable, lowly selves - but very confused as to why she was thanking them.

Finally, someone who seemed to be the mayor put up his hand, "Ah, Oracle?" Meridius looked up and nodded for him to talk. "Why are you thanking us for doing whatever it is we do?"

"Well," she explained, "if you DIDN'T do what you did, who else would? So, if you didn't do what you do, nothing would get done!"

The logic was irrefutable. After all, they were the only ones in the village who did what they did. Considering this notion deeply, every one of the peasants was amazed to discover they were much happier doing whatever it was that they did, and SOME were even proud of what they didn't. The gloom and misery of their daily existence evaporated and they became suffused with a buoyant delight. Because now, doing whatever it was they did now offered them great hope for the future that they could continue doing exactly that.

This was simply more proof of her divine wisdom and all agreed that this act of genius notched up yet another miracle by the Oracle!

oooO000ooo

A scene of bustling commerce greeted the travelers as they arrived at the gates to Delphi. Rising above them in the background, Mount Parnassus gazed down impassively at the traders and merchants cashing in on gullible tourists.

"Fox hats, get your Fox Hats!" a vendor shouted as they wheeled through into the sacred compound.

Meridius looked a little puzzled, "They used to sell protective amulets."

"What did people need protection from?" Asked Rufus.

"Oh, seasickness, snakes, all the usual stuff," she answered.

"Did they work?"

"On snakes, yes, that is if you were quick enough and you had bought the correct protection amulet - one that was sharp enough and long enough, you know, like a sword. Protection against spiders are shorter, flatter amulets, making it much easier to swat them." Then she leaned over and chatted to some passerby, "The Ogoglio?" she asked.

The fellow, who appeared to be a Parthian by the strange manner of dress, nodded and gestured up ahead, as if to say, "Up there!" But you had to assume this is what he meant, for he gave no indication of what was actually up there, other than something.

This is part of the curious nature of Parthians, their ambient gestures and non-committal sense of vagueness were, by report, a religious thing for them. The other thing they were famous for was a complete and utter lack of interest in statues, either of Gods or famous people, which possibly explains the paucity of monuments in their home cities. Some historians will one day look back and say this is why they didn't last as a culture, but the truth is that a society based on gestures is not particularly good at withstanding sandstorms nor the vagaries of time.

Despite the Parthian utter lack of conviction in the importance of statuary, Delphi was still the place where everyone put up a monument and in this instance, the Parthians did get into the spirit of things, almost - They put up a street lamp, saying it was a sacred tripod to Apollo. Which was passably strange, because it was one-legged - but it DID have three snakes at the top, so if you turned it upside down you would get the notion of a tripod. The question was never raised as to what use an upside down street lamp might be, but this did not detract from the three legged snakishness - thus tripodishness - of its embellishments.

Some suspected it was not a monument at all, but just a street lamp put up in the Parthian section because it was dark at night and Parthians hated being mugged. However, I am sure you would agree that questions over what makes a statue are a bit like arguments over art. If you want to call a frame full of fallen leaves the 'Art of Autumn', no one has the right to gainsay it. So it WAS a monument and given that Parthians were monumentally fond of the lack of said edifices, the street lamp was therefore paradoxically a MORE significant gift to the Gods - or, in other words, a halfway decent attempt to appease the Romans so as to stop them running into Parthia and stealing all their gold.

Rufus had at this point said very little, as his general demeanor towards Delphi and its statues was more Parthian than Greek. The whole place was a bit dull and, other than the years when they ran the Delphic Games, he saw little point in it. Yet this tiny town on the cliffs above the Corinthian Gulf had become the center of worship for the entire world and for some reason people kept erecting monuments here. Every tiny victory by some marginal leader in a far-off province was given the divine stamp of approval when the King or Viceroy who organized it commemorated his win by dedicating a monument at Delphi.

Alternatively, people like the Parthians put up a street lamp as a sort of protection statue, that told the Romans they were getting into the swing of things and didn't need to be invaded, I mean, educated.

To this end, the place was now a MONUMENTAL clutter of monuments, statues, and votary shines, made even worse by all the traders selling little miniature versions of the same to tourists. Every square inch of the place had something poking up that declared a victory over someone, somewhere for some reason, and thanking God for it.

And what God did they thank? Their OWN of course. And here is a curious point, no one ever thanked the God of the defeated opponents for failing to be a particularly effective deity. No, it was always, "The God of the Ethiopians is thanked for the mighty victory over whoever it might be".

Honestly, as far as Rufus was concerned it only served to prove the Parthians had the right idea. No monuments, other than useful things like street lamps. They had now reached the point where they had to leave their cart, as the roads were so full of tribute sculptures and people selling earwax candles for burning in the sacred shrines, that there was no more room for a donkey cart. But he had to ask the question that had been niggling him - he knew he didn't want to ask this, and presumed he wouldn't like the answer, but he had to ask, "Meridian darling, what is an Ogoglio?"

"Oh," she murmured, "A sort of stand-in. My brother."

"I didn't know you had family." Ofal, who was almost revived from his seasickness and no longer constantly throwing up into a bucket, seemed oddly pleased with this.

"I have you, darlings," she noted.

Rufus felt a deep sense of pride swelling in his chest with this comment. The Oracle considered him family! His chest puffed out in pride but as he did so, she looked at him with an exasperated look, "No more Ogoglio, PLEASE!" she exclaimed.

He had no idea what the problem was, or what she meant, or what was Ogoglioish about him, but he felt extremely deflated, which seemed to make her happy - so he 'sort of' cheered up. "I still don't even know what an Ogoglio is, and now it sounds like something I don't want to, anyway," he said, disconsolately thinking of how much more fun Corinth would be.

As they picked their way through the never-ending parade of monuments and shrines and triumphal obelisks, they finally made it to what was a rather odd looking building. It was a square, dull affair, especially compared to the magnificent Temple of Apollo beside it, but it had a small sign pointing towards a door that had a carved stone sign that said, "ORACLE THIS WAY". Rufus peered in and beyond the entrance, he saw a staircase that led downwards. The next sign that appeared as they entered the portico was a roughly painted affair with the words, "Ogoglio - Down Here!" written on it.

"This is where the Ogoglio would be then?" Rufus asked rhetorically.

"Mmmm,' was all Meridius said.

Ofal went up to the door and wrinkled his nose as the fumes of sulfur hit him. "Smells like Hades in there!"

But on top of that was an array of expensive perfumes, and many people wearing fox hats. All seemed to be crowded around something in the darkness and there was a general muttering and a mootering with a distinct flavor of money on top of it all. This was where the wealthy leaders of the world gathered to hear what the Oracle said of their particular situation.

Meridius said nothing and just stood there, waiting. Finally, a priest came up to them with application forms, and when he recognized whose presence he was in his eyes opened wide and he fell prostrate on the ground. With a groveling whine, he exclaimed with excited relief, "Oh great Oracle, we had no idea! At last! At Last! We are all so damn sick of your brother!"

"Mmmm,' was all Meridius said.

The priest made a loud whistle. Heads turned, then many more sets of eyes recognized who was back, and they, too, fell prostrate on the ground, muttering words that sounded an awful lot like, "Finally, we can piss off the Ogoglio!"

"Mmmm,' was all Meridius said.

Rufus saw waves of people begin to gather around, shouting, "Thank the GODS she is BACK!" The same citizens who, only ten seconds ago, had barely noticed them were now all falling to the ground, crying out how glad they were to see her.

Ofal laughed, thinking he was being clever like Rufus, and made a funny comment, saying, "We got a prostrate problem here I think."

Of course, no one laughed, which was entirely appropriate, as he was an unfunny comedian.

On the Road to Delphi

The Ogoglio

D own the stairs the troupe went, Meridius in front, Ofal and Rufus behind, and following them while somehow managing to bow and scrape all at the same time, were the throngs of priests and temple functionaries, still murmuring praises to Apollo for the safe return of the Divine One.

"Is Bette Midlus performing here?" Ofal asks Rufus.

"Why would she be performing in Delphi?" Rufus asked, astonished at this odd question.

"They keep talking about the divine one, which everyone knows is Bette Midlus."

"Idiot," snapped back Rufus, "HERE the Divine One is Meridius."

Oh," said Ofal, as if he understood. "I didn't know she sang."

Rufus shook his head, while Meridius appeared to hear nothing - but she was listening FOR something. As they made their way down, a soft moaning could be heard - the religious type of noise which is not the 'damn that hurts' moan but a sort of 'woe is me' entreaty to the Gods.

As their eyes adjusted to the darkness, they made out the faint outline of some governmental ruler standing before a chasm, with a fellow sitting there on a tripod, making guttural sounds. As they got closer they watched as an official made their way forward, obviously petitioning for an answer to some vexing question.

A man sitting on the tripod above a chasm asked, "Where are you from?"

The fellow replied, "Attica Minor"

To which the fellow sighed and said, "Wear the Fox Hat!"

So the Attica Minor fellow explained, "It is just to the North a few hundred leagues, then West a thousand or so. Roads are terrible, wine is good."

"NO!" shouted the man on the tripod. I said WEAR THE FOX HAT! Are you stupid?"

The government official started to moan and abase himself and say how lowly he was and could the Ogoglio ever forgive him?

It seemed that before them sat the Ogoglio! The government official was still there next to the Oracle's tripod, moaning, as they wandered in. Finally, Meridius breaks up the scene by speaking, "Ogoglio darling, why are all they moaning?"

"Oh thank the GODS you are back. I am SO DAMN BORED by these idiots. All these thick-as-three-bricks priests and stupid, stupid people, they understand NOTHING! I tell them the obvious, I give them the simple truth, but they seem to think it is some divinely inspired pronouncement and try to understand the mystery behind it. In all truth, if I wasn't so UTTERLY GORGEOUS and WONDERFUL I would have done myself in by now." he said, in terms that seemed to indicate he thought rather highly of himself.

"But I don't, of course. After all, I am such a MAGNIFICENT PIECE of ALPHA MALE! How could I deprive the world of ME? It would be an utter crime to humanity itself if I removed myself, but I tell you Meridius, you can only take so much," he appeared to conclude.

'Brother dear," Meridius sighed, "Why are you here?"

"Why else!" he exclaimed in a booming voice not dissimilar to their erstwhile companion, Brutus Maximus. "I am here to give them the warning and to tell them to wear the fox hat!"

Meridius was restraining herself, "But dearest brother, why are you telling people to wear fox hats?"

"Because of the WEREWOLVES, of course. Didn't you realize? They are out of Hades and eating everything and everyone they can, but if they think you are a relative, they leave you alone."

"Ohhh," said Meridius, getting the picture. "You didn't think of calling up Zeusey-boo and asking him to sort it out?"

The Ogoglio shuffled his feet, suddenly appearing to turn a vague shade of shy. "Zeus is somewhat snappish with me, darling. He even told me to shut up last time we were chatting. Can you imagine, telling me to shut up? I was in the middle of explaining the difference between Newton's Laws of Gravity and the effect it has after the thirteenth bottle of beer and he told me to put a sock in it! Well, yes - Maybe I did call him a boring old fart - which was about the same time I started ducking the lightning bolts and clearing out of Olympus."

Meridius just shook her head. He was SO exasperating. "No matter brother dearest, I am back and I will look into it."

The gaggle of officials, priests, and nere-do-wells that had followed her in hung there expectantly, apparently waiting for the Ogoglio to clear out. How it was possible for a single human being to manage to annoy so many people without even trying, we may never know, but it was certain that, as much as Meridius was loved, her brother was detested.

As a curiosity, she paused to ask him, "Ah, why did you turn up in the first place?"

"My DEAR sister - Werewolves! I was getting tired of having to kill them so I came over to ask YOU to intercede with Zeus ... But you were off in the new world, the stool was empty, so I sat down to wait for you, and THEN all these people so desperate for answers started asking ME. Well, I decided the Gods wanted me to warn them about the werewolves, and yes - I know as the Oracle you are not SUPPOSED to give a simple direct answer and just generalized clues, but when it is so cut and dried, what are you supposed to do? The fox hat solves the problem!"

"My dearest brother, you are not an Oracle, you are a carpenter who was too lazy to build your own house. Are you certain all this wasn't about free rent and board?" she queried.

The Ogoglio seemed to be affronted by such a suggestion and spluttered, "Not at all, or at least, not all of it was that. It was quite fun to be in the Oracle chair, except for all the stupid people." He glared out at the rather angry looking throng who had gathered, annoyed that he admitted his advice that was completely lacking in decent obtuseness, such as, *"On the crest of the moon, donkeys will laugh and the tide will be blue!"* and such-like.

People put up with a lot and citizens tend to be mostly easy to get on with things, but bad prophecy was something no one could abide. And the Ogoglio's prophecies were exceedingly bad. There was no, "Trust to your wooden walls!" from him. When pressed with any serious question it was just, "Wear the Fox Hat!". They were done with him and wanted this pretender to the throne out of there.

It was a communication problem where exceedingly GOOD advice was being given in a far too direct manner. As everyone currently had a problem with werewolves, wearing a fox hat was indeed excellent and sage wisdom - but the priestly populace thought it too blunt, positively gauche, and was having none of it.

Rufus was a past master at knowing when a crowd was about to attack and judged that this would be right about now. "I say, Meridius. As you are settled in here, I was thinking I should take the Ogoglio here and head off to some bars in Corinth. What you reckon?"

"Mmmm," she agreed (or at least appeared to agree).

"Excellent, well old chap, let's go get drunk!" he grabbed the Ogoglio from his tripod and, pulling him aside, whispered, "They are going to kill you, possibly me as well, and potentially everyone bar Meridius, so we had better clear out."

The great and glorious Ogoglio was entirely unaware and thus exceedingly ungrateful that the sudden appearance of his sister probably saved him from being murdered by that crowd, but regardless of this fact, this fine fellow mentioned drinking! That seemed a far better use of his time than sitting with these dull creatures, so he was happy to leave. The priests breathed a sigh of relief, they had Meridius back and the Ogoglio was now on his way out the door - This was deemed to be a reasonable arrangement by the mob, so Rufus was able to elbow his way through the still tense and angry peasantry and get themselves onto a donkey cart down to Kirra, to catch a boat to Corinth.

Meridius just sighed and stepped back into her old role, which was giving advice in the most obtuse manner possible to all the government officials who came to get a pronouncement of their fate. But Werewolves? She really would have to put in a call to Daddy-boos - they were not a thing to be taken lightly.

Ofal could see she was back on the tripod, so he tagged along with Rufus and the strange fellow called the Ogoglio, and the three of them headed off to the bars of Corinth.

Beautiful Downtown Corinth

CORINTH

Beautiful Corinth, glorious Corinth, star of the Aegean - replete with marble-faced houses, streets wider than a donkey cart, ocean breezes to cool the heat of a Greek summer, loads of hookers, and bars stocked with quite decent wine. Heaven itself, unless you were a Christian. That was the strangest thing about that cult, everything good they said was bad, and everything bad they said was good. Luxury was evil, while a wooden shack full of prickles was somehow good, for it reminded them of the suffering of the Lord. Who worships suffering? Most rightly considered the Christians to be entirely mad.

Corinth was the antithesis to pain - It was a marvelous place, with ancient culture jumbled up with modern life, where archaic traditions mixed with the latest wine making technology. Corinth was all things that made life amenable for delightful, drunken debauchery in the moonlight followed by sweet, slothful, slumbering somnambulance in the park during the day.

The only thorn in the side were those incredibly annoying Christians who would wake you up from your bliss in the sun and start proselytizing about their prophet who said love was the best thing a man could find - yet this was a lie because they never went to the hookers! It made absolutely no sense, these killjoys who said having fun was bad and suffering was good were terribly dull - Yet they had lots of followers. Probably because they gave free food and lodging to thieves and convicts, thought Rufus - But so typical, in a city where love was the main stock in trade, the Christians only talked about it or said you had to be married to get it. This was how insane they were, thinking that getting married to someone improved your love life!

However, if you ignored the Christians and their annoying habit of trying to convert you, Corinth was the perfect world for Rufus and, as it turned out, the Ogoglio.

It wasn't that Rufus was HAPPY Meridius was busy in Delphi, or that she cramped their style, but both Ofal and Rufus knew her idea of tremendous fun involved sorting out a jigsaw, not being spread-eagled on a wall as a dartboard for a hundred drunken mercenaries. She was not really the type to encourage a raunchy time. In point of fact, when the working girls met with the Oracle, they went prostrate in a very non-sexual manner and stopped working. Her brother, however, had quite the opposite effect. Turning up with the Ogoglio in tow meant that the party had come to town!

The lads started knocking back the vino on the boat, bought some more on the wharf, and laughed in a meaningless, carousing sort of cheer all the way into town as they sat in the donkey cart they hired at the exorbitant wharf prices. The Ogoglio explained, "You need the cart because without it, getting between brothels when you are legless is just impossible. And talking about getting legless, that bar over there looks like a fine establishment to start the celebrations!"

The Sitting Duck, it was called - a simple bar that looked like it had that most important of all ingredients to make a good time, alcohol and strange looking people.

Sitting outside, having a rather aggressive conversation with a philosopher, were seven dwarves, called (according to their name tags) Itchy, Bitchy, Sweaty, Sleepy, Bloated, Forgetful, and Psycho. But instead of Snow White, there was a rather garish fellow sitting with them, drinking happily and apparently disinterested in anything his short-arsed companions had to say. This stuck Rufus as a good indication of a thoroughly decent chap, so he went up to say hello.

"Do you mind, it seems to me that you are dressed like a pimp, yet you are sitting here with dwarves? Is there some sort of strange trade in dwarf sex here we don't know about?"

The pimp looked up, "Oh god no. These little monsters are clients that seem to think an argument is as important as sex - I am just keeping them busy until I can get them back to my brothel." The fellow made tasteless an understatement, wearing a bright yellow and red check jacket, striped blue and green pants, and a rather expensive paisley silk shirt. None of which went together in any way at all, and yet when confronted with this opposition of harmony - it seemed to work.

Rufus smiled broadly - base, uncouth fellows like this were always an indicator of a good time. "Excellent - just what we were looking for. Rufus is my name, this smelly looking fellow is Ofal, and the extremely arrogant, very drunk man with us is the Ogoglio," he said, proffering a hand in friendship.

At the sound of that word, the good people in the tavern looked up with delight, shouting, "The Ogoglio!" and raised a mighty cheer, and drinks were on the house. This was, Rufus surmised, the sort of drinking buddy you want.

The pimp however merely dipped his head as if acknowledging new clients rather than a Demi-god and shook their hand, saying, "I am known as Seachell Caruthers, with a 'c'."

"A 'C' as in Carruthers not spelled with a 'K'?" Rufus asked.

"No you fool, Caruthers is always spelled with a 'C' - The 'C' is instead of the 'S' in the 'shell' part of Seachell," Seachell explained with a rather testy annoyance.

Ofal was perplexed, "I would have thought the "C" should be in the "sea" part of Seashell. Though I suppose you could double it up and have 'C-c-hell'?" he enquired, though his question was more to his own dull brain than anyone present.

Seachell just looked skywards, obviously having had this discussion too many times in the past. He then started bringing out a long pointy thing, very much like the amulet for protection against snakes, apparently intending to prod Ofal with it.

While beating back the urge to ask why any of this spelling business was important, Rufus soothed the potentially ruffled water. "My friend, be at ease! We are not here to argue, unlike your dwarves here. We are just looking for booze and girls, without didactic arguments over letters as they are or they are not... "

Rufus had his sentence rudely snipped by a furious looking dwarf, who exclaimed, "Existentialist rubbish!"

"Pardon?" asked Rufus, feeling somewhat butted in on.

"Whether we are or we are not! We are discussing the self-evident reality, whether tis nobler in the Soul to cope with the arrows and slings of outrageous fortune or to get a large stick and sort the matter!"

Another drunken dwarf barged in on the conversation no one was having. "Or maybe wash, as the case may be," he added while snubbing a nose at Ofal.

"We weren't discussing that!" objected Ofal.

Another Dwarf turns from his argument with a patron, to argue the contrary, pointing his finger at Ofal, "No? Then why are you here denying it! Sounds like you are part of the discussion to me."

Ofal propped up and was about to say, *"No I wasn't!"* when he realized the downright sneakiness of the Dwarves, but before he could think of something clever to say, Seachell took over.

"Now now, gentlemen," Seachell soothed the increasing turbulence of Dwarves who were winding up for an all-out verbal assault on the newcomers. "Didactic imperialism and alternative nihilistic 'isms of any particular flavor are not what our friends are here for. They want to go to the Brothel. Ah - (He looks at the trio standing there) Who did you say you were again?"

Rufus was pleased someone had taken charge of the rampaging dwarves and bowed saying, "Eruptus Non-Funnius at your service."

It had the effect of a rather large pin dropping. The little folk all stopped yabbering and stared at the trio. They then hurriedly started whispering and discussing amongst themselves the ramifications and one - evidently the leader - spoke up, saying, "If you are Eruptus Non-Funnius, where is the Delphic Oracle?"

"Well, in Delphi, of course. But we have a substitute, her brother, the Ogoglio." Rufus explained.

This caused a VERY large pin to drop. There was a sort of stunned silence and then all the dwarves fell to their knees (a very strange thing considering standing upright they were roughly the same heights as a person already on their knees) exclaiming, "All praise to the Ogoglio!"

Rufus was confused, asking Seachell, "Didn't they just hear the entire bar shout 'The Ogoglio!'?"

To which the dwarves groveled just a little bit more and shouted, "All praise to the Ogoglio!"

Seachell shrugged, "There is a race called Japanese. They have paper-thin walls but they cannot hear anyone on the other side of that paper, even if the people there are having wild, exuberant sex. The dwarves have something similar in that they pay no attention to the coarse stupidity of the proletariat but you made mention that you were connected to something of importance, therefore raising the possibility of networking. Well, this gets their attention," he explained.

The already extremely drunk Ogoglio appeared not to notice and staggered over to a table where a flagon of beer appeared to be demanding his attention. This seemed to break the spell, and suddenly all the little folk began jabbering at an incredible rate of knots, speaking in some high pitched language that only they understood.

At this point, Seachell Caruthers pulled out what seemed to be a glass rectangle, and put his ear to it, nodding as he did so. This rather intrigued Rufus, so he asked what he was doing.

Slo-Mo glass," Seachell explained. "It slows down the speed of sound, and light for that matter, so I can understand what they are saying." He could see the confused look on the face of Rufus, so he went up and put the glass block to the fellows ear.

Rufus was astonished. What had seemed a stream of high pitched squeals and squeaks was now a discernable conversation. What a remarkable invention! And what he heard was surprising - Apparently, the Dwarves hated Zeus and because the Ogoglio was hated BY Zeus, he had therefore achieved a sort of Godhood in their curious religion - which was multi-level marketing, a faith best described as having everything to do about nothing while have little to about anything.

He had heard of it some time ago, and even read the famous book on the dark science of MLM, entitled, "How to lose friends and influence nobody."

Finally one of the strange fellows stopped yabbering, and stood forward, asking, "How did you duck the lightning bolts, oh Great Ogoglio?"

The Ogoglio looked incredibly disinterested, "Oh, luck I guess. What is IMPORTANT is that we leave this bar and find a brothel."

"Hang about," a familiar, inveterately cheery voice bellowed from somewhere across the street - "Did someone say the magic word?" And so it was that unwelcomed, uninvited, and entirely unaware of this fact, Brutus Maximus also joined the tribe. Let's not discuss the detail that no one said the magic word, which was 'alcohol', but you would have to admit, the mention of a bar or a brothel meant pretty much the same thing.

Finally, the light of interest came to the Ogoglio's eyes. "Herc baby - wonderful to catch up, it's been centuries."

Brutus Maximus strode into view, smiling broadly, "Ogoglio old chap - I truly can't remember the last time but this is because I have had this memory lapse thing. I even forgot I was Hercules, can you believe?" he roared while embracing the hapless fellow in a bear hug.

The eyes of the dwarves grew even wider, "Hercules!" they all whispered in awe. "Hercules AND the Ogoglio!" they then murmured with a sort of religious fervor. "Ah, gentlemen, we have a wonderful business opportunity we want to discuss with you."

Christians Blocking Business

The crew made their way happily to the brothel of Seachell Caruthers, laughing and drinking, with the dwarves hanging off the cart discussing how they will all be incredibly rich, when they were strangely confronted with a large group of very unhappy looking Christians, who surrounded the brothel of Seachell with a protest, bearing signs saying "The End is Nigh" and "Fornification is the Devils Work!"

Rufus had to look twice, and with incredible foolishness, he found himself asking, "Don't you mean Fornication? I am not sure Fornification is a word."

At which the entire cluster of them turned and pointed, saying, "It's the devil! It's the DEVIL!" And when Seachell went to move the cart around them, they started shouting, "They are going in to Fornificate! Fornificators all!"

The Christians then menacingly crowded round the cart, pointing and accusing them all of fornification and being the devil. Brutus Maximus, Hercules to his friends, was confused, "Pan isn't here, is he?"

However unwise it might be to corral someone like Hercules and shout abuse in his direction, the Christians appeared to be very focused on not allowing anyone into Seachell's brothel, which was situated on a lovely beachfront part of Corinth, and had a marvelous sign out the front that read, "Seachell's Brothel - He sells She Sells by the Sea Shore".

The wise brothel owner just pushed through the Christians, using the sharp, long thing he was going to use on Ofal at the bar. It was very effective, and quite a few fell to the ground wailing in pain. "Do you always have to do this, getting to your place of business?" Rufus asked.

"Oh yes," explained Seachell. "They are all just crazy fools who preach love but try to stop everyone from getting some. I have petitioned the clerk of the courts to have them removed, but he says there are so many of them that as soon as they move on one mob, another lot will come to take their place. Honestly, they are worse than mad cat women"

"Don't they get upset over you jabbing them like this?" Rufus was amazed, for he currently expected a riot followed by a great deal of bloodshed and was thinking the unthinkable, that he was happy Brutus was with them.

"No, apparently not. I have even accidentally killed a few, but when I said I was sorry, they all said it was OK and that it was their job to forgive me. So I just prod away, but even so, it is not good for business -

This is why I have the wagon and have to amuse annoying creatures like dwarves so I can drum up customers." Seachell explained with a sigh.

Ofal thought it was very strange, "How come they are here anyway? Don't they want everyone to get on? Every other religion in Rome is all about getting along with each other, despite the fact that anyone not on your side is wrong and corrupt."

There was, apparently, no answer to this conundrum.

The Ogoglio and Brutus were having a chat about Olympus and the latest gossip and appeared not to notice the bodies falling to one side as the cart plowed through them. Their collective oblivion concerning the matters of humans was not so much that everyone else in the cart was less than them, that was a given, it was more that mere humans didn't live long enough to warrant any form of deep discussion. Humans, fragile as they were, just fell over in old age before they got to any worthwhile answer to any decent question. They needed to have discussions that lasted generations, and to do this they had to record their arguments into very long scrolls so that they could give these arguments to their children so that the next generation could continue the conversation they did not have the time to finish.

Rufus, on the other hand, was concerned about the length of his life in an entirely different way: He wanted to see the end of it in old age, not with a sign stuck in his chest that ironically said 'The End is Nigh'. He mused, "You know, what we need is a way to sort out whose God is the best. Just as we have our Olympic Games, I think we should have something like the Mount Olympus Games, where the GODS compete, to see who is the top dog."

A roaring thunder breached the noise of the Christians, a tumult of brimstone evacuated from Hades and spewed over Pompey (again) and lightning flashed in the sky on what had been a perfect, cloudless day.

And back in Delphi, Meridius sat upright on her tripod and exclaimed, "The Mount Olympus Games!"

Valhalla

Odin's all-seeing eye had been kept busy this last week, watching all the other Gods and what they were up to. Thor was drinking with Loki as they listened to his plans, "We have to win this lads," he said. "We have been losing market share to the Romans, and we need something to shift public opinion our way."

To be fair, neither Loki nor Thor were all that concerned. If the rest of Europe wanted to follow the Roman Gods, who cared? The Roman Worship Quotient was so diluted with the hundreds of faiths in Rome that even a ten percent rating for the Nordic Gods was sufficient to sustain their godliness, and they were still in the twenties.

Their general look of disinterest annoyed Odin, and he bellowed at them, "By the immortal power of lightning I would have both of you chained to a rock. Do you not understand anything? You are content to sit there drinking mead, thinking highly of yourselves, but Zeus is planning to bury us! I can feel it in my bones, this game they are setting up is in deadly earnest. One God will rule supreme, while the rest of us are cast into Niflheim - I have seen it!"

"Have you been down to Hades, father?" Thor asked. "It's quite lovely, and Hades himself is the perfect gentleman. The only thing that unsettles him is the mention of Zeus, he hates his brother. A little bit like Loki and myself, except we enjoy a drink or three and don't take our hatred personally."

"Fools!" shouted Odin. "You all seem to think these games are just sport, but underneath there is a dark secret that even I cannot explain. My ravens hear the whispers, my bones speak to me of treachery, but I cannot discern the shape of it. Loki, I want you to go see Zeus, make him think you are a beautiful woman. When he falls in love, he can't help himself, he will do whatever you suggest - so slip him a Gravity Pill. While he is weak, get him to tell you his secret. He will blab like a baby.

"And you, Thor, I want you to go see Vulcan. Tell him you have always wanted to be a blacksmith, and that you have the hammer for it - ask him to teach you the dark arts of creating weapons for the Gods."

Thor snorted, "Vulcan is a pile of misery disguised as a God. I don't know he could stand having my cheery nature around, though I will admit to a fascination with how he shaped weapons like Excalibur."

"I have foreseen he will accept you, but only if he genuinely believes you want to learn his art. Do not be fooled my children, Vulcan is older than all of us. He was around with the forming of the sun and the shaping of the worlds into order - he has the blood of chaos in his veins. And he is up to something - you need to discover what." Odin stared into the distance.

"Father, are you sure? I will happily go and do as you ask, for his work is truly the greatest forging ever wrought, but he is also a jealous God. He may not want to let me go once he accepts an apprentice." Thor looked up from his mead, it was an intriguing proposition.

"Nothing your hammer can't sort if it comes to that. Off you pair go, I don't want to see your lazy arses around here until we have some real information on what is up."

What WASN'T up were the poll numbers. For the last hundred years, all the Gods had been slowly drifting down in the belief factor as humans started to think for themselves and realize they did not need gods to achieve their ends. The Norse Gods were doing better than most, but the Vikings had all gotten into business suits and were selling IKEA while singing ABBA songs. Odin's family were becoming token Gods at best, and given another hundred years of disinterest, belief in the Gods would fail.

WHY is this important? Despite their supposed immortality, Gods need worship and respect to maintain it. The FAITH of the people was their fuel, one that gave the Gods their raison d'être. But now, rich humans were taking over the role of worship, without any understanding of what it meant, and how it empowered you. People were starting to worship money, and any who had money were being regarded as a sort of God.

Despite his one eye, Odin had a clear view of the long haul. The Gods were becoming irrelevant, especially now that animal sacrifice had largely been abandoned. Humans did not know it, but the spilling of blood stirred their most primitive state, that of the killer ape. It was not the animals that were important, nor the killing of them, it was the vibrant energy that emerged from the killer ape, the creature that dreamed of murder and mayhem. This is what radiated out and fed the Gods for the very act of death affirmed the faith of the humans, and gave forth the energy that sustained all of them.

It was that damn Oracle that started the process of their downfall. She was heart and soul of this movement and at the center of everything that was wrong. Plus, the fact she was a personal favorite of Zeus was not a thing to be taken lightly. To Odin it was clear, Zeus was engineering the removal of all of them. He just had to discover how the plot was being written for their demise and he knew with a deep certainty that Vulcan was involved.

Soon he would find out, but in the meantime, sit and wait. These games were very obviously part and parcel of this great plan, so he would go along as if he thought it was all a good idea, and then kybosh their plans and see if he can't restore the role of Valhalla as the premium place of worship.

After Loki and Thor left for their appointed duties, a scribe came up, and begged an audience, "Sire, great Odin, greatest of all the Gods - you have a visitor."

"Jesus Christ," he says to the walls.

The scribe was astonished at the all-seeing eye of the great one, "Exactly, your greatness."

Jesus Meets Odin

Despite Odin's initial displeasure at the visit, turns out that this Christ fellow was not too bad. He loved a good mead and was a fantastic storyteller. They would stay up late into the summer nights, in the days of perpetual sunlight, where Jesus would regale him with a thousand different stories of this peasant or that knight, and on and on he went.

In two whole months, not one repeated story, and as long as he was occasionally crucified (to work out the creaks) he was always good for another one. You may not like Christians, let's face it, NO ONE liked Christians, but Jesus himself was an absolute hoot. Odin found he far preferred his company to that of his overly proud sons. "It's not that they are arrogant," he slurred after his sixteenth barrel of mead, "it's just that they are so full of themselves. I mean, I have a life as well, you know. But no, they don't want to hear how I beat the great serpent. Kids, what can you do?"

"In all truth," Jesus replied, matching Odin mead for mead, "My father doesn't like me much. I mean, let's face it - he sent me down to be crucified. I like you, Odin, the only person YOU sacrifice is yourself, and I respect that," he slurred in return.

Odin shook his head, "You are a great kid," he said, meaning it. "No, really - a great kid. Any father would be proud of you, and I have to respect how well you can hold your drink."

Jesus just held up his hand in agreement. "Hey, my people founded a whole religion on how well you can hold your drink. My followers drink wine and bless them, they think they are drinking MY BLOOD! Can you believe it? My BLOOD!"

"Damn," said Odin, "That is almost Viking. I am impressed, Jesus. We are a lot alike, you and I. I mean, yes I don't mind sacrificing virgins and all that, but UNDERNEATH this, we are not so very different. So what is it that brings you up here?"

Jesus laughs, looking out on the frozen wastes of Valhalla, "Well, it's not the climate, that's for sure!" he jests.

Odin smiles, and is suddenly dead sober, "No really, why are you here?"

Jesus just nods, "I am glad you asked. I don't want to impose my view on your people, I do not want to change your religion in any way, and I do not want to influence you with sweet talking or bribes, but it seems to me that by joining forces we become a far more powerful tool."

"How so?" Odin asked, genuinely curious about what is on offer.

"Well, you know we have Christmas? Twenty-Fifth December, supposedly the day I was born, which is a tad ridiculous because I was born in April. Well, we did this because it slotted in to the existing beliefs. We all know the REAL Santa Clause was Odin leading the Wild Hunt across the world during the midwinter period, riding on his flying, eight-legged horse, Sleipnir. All WE did was superimpose the notion of Santa and reindeer, but it is the same myth. You see, our people are ALREADY worshipping you, just under a different name.

"Facts are, we have taken every feast day in our faith from one of the old world. Remember Eostre, the Celtic Goddess of fertility? She became our Easter. We literally do not have a feast day that is ours - It is all borrowed. We are a jigsaw religion, a mishmash of what everyone believes, with our notions put over the top. Now before you scoff, it works. We absorb the faiths of others and make them our own - The point is, this WORKS. We still have fervent believers, we still have loads of belief energy. What we do NOT have is relevance or respect." Jesus looked up at Odin.

The ancient God nodded, he was liking where this was going. "So you are thinking a sort of merger? A mix between the two faiths? How would this work out?"

"Well, I thought it was obvious. Your people already call you father, my people also call my dad 'the father'. Which is sad, because he is a miserable old bastard who has wiped whole cities and turned people into salt, not exactly a nice guy. The truth is, I would prefer to call you Dad."

"I already got sons, Jesus. How does this work?"

"I got nothing against Thor, he is a great bloke. And man, he can drink, you have to respect a guy who can drink like that. So I got no problem with Thor, but let's face it, they worship him as thunder, and everyone knows, the cause of thunder is lightning. That is YOUR shtick."

"Jesus, Jesus, Jesus," Odin muses, "all your people call you the only begotten son. You can't just turn up with brothers all of a sudden."

"I got that covered, we make Thor the Holy Spirit, Loki becomes Satan, you become the holy father, I am the son. It will work, and everyone has a role to play."

"You got the demon-graphics for this?" Odin asked, squinting his eyes because he was kind of liking this concept. "

"In the modern world, we call it demo-graphics. And yes, I do - the combined potential of BOTH our faiths is hitting thirty nine percent. This is a higher faith quotient than all the Roman and Greek Gods combined, and our side is a growing statistic. My prediction is that if we join forces in a friendly merger, we will hit fifty percent."

"Interesting, but my people are called Pagans by your people. They pretty must hate each other, how are you going to make that work?" Odin liked the notion of fifty percent, though.

"I am not saying it will be easy, but the thing is, both our people share a love of one thing, drinking. I mean, Vikings and Christians are already brothers of the booze, so we imply that the wine that is MY blood is also YOUR sacrifice - that's all we need do, then trust their need to drink. And let's also face it, Loki would love to be called Satan. I mean, he already has the horns..." (Jesus was kind enough not to question the patrimony of the mischievous son)

Odin leaned back, considering things deeply. "In all my years I had never considered a merger, but you could be right. The way to reinforce the bottom line is always more followers and believers, and with this plan we can invigorate both paths. Plus, let's face it, your people are a little uptight about sex and a good bonking with some of our Viking women will transform their worldview."

"As long as they are married," interjected Jesus.

"As long as they can get divorced," responded Odin.

"Fair call," Jesus nodded. "So, this can work?"

Odin stepped down from his throne, and shook the hand of the savior, saying, "This can work!"

"Fantastic!" beamed Jesus, throwing some nails onto the table. "Now, do you mind putting me up for the night? I need a bit of a stretch."

Loki Meets Zeus

Knowing how the old Greed God had a penchant for pretty girls, Loki surrounded himself in an azure veil of beauty, and spoke to it, saying, "I am now the most beautiful woman in the world!" In a show of powerful magic, the veil took shape and conformed to the image of Helen of Troy. Loki could feel the change, and as the magic seeped into every orifice, it created a new one!

THAT was unexpected! His voice then became higher, and his chest began to puff out. In moments, there he was, completely transformed into an amazingly beautiful woman, standing outside the house of Garam Marsala. He tinkled the bell and some slave came to the door, "Is Zeus in?" Loki asked in a sultry voice.

Hearing the lustrous tone automatically pricked up the ears of every male in earshot. Baraka Alashad was walking past, and stopped, going to the door and inviting the stunning creature he found therein. "And what might YOUR name be my dear?" he asked.

Now, if this were a man or even a horned creature like Loki, the question would have been, "What do you want?" but as every man there already knew what they wanted when they looked at her, the only other question they had in mind was, "How do I chat this gorgeous thing up?"

Loki found himself (or herself as the case was) feeling quite chuffed at the attention. With all this adulation suddenly flowing his way he even felt that losing the Sky Falling Worshippers from Gaul was no great loss at all. He/she basked in the attention flowing at him/her and felt that maybe he was of the wrong sex. He had NO idea how much power a beautiful woman had to attract faith energy! He/she fluttered his/her eyes, and said in that deep come hither tone that the truly stunning woman perfects, "I am here to see Zeus..."

At which point the roaring of the great God was self-evident, for he had emptied yet another bottle of wine and was demanding another. A harried Garam Marsala came up from the basement looking stressed and anxious, until he saw the radiant creature in their midst, "Oh, and who might YOU be?" he asked adoringly.

Loki just smiled, held out her hand to be kissed, which they all did with tremendous eagerness, and requested, "Zeus?"

Garam unplugged his eyes from her breasts, shook himself free of his madness, and indicated the stairs where he had emerged from. "Down there?" she/he asked, understanding that the poor fellow had been struck dumb. Garam nodded speechlessly in the affirmative. "Thank you SO much darlings," said Loki as she/he swanned past them, calling out, "Zeussy baby?"

Wearing a stunning gold encrusted gown, split to the hip to show the bronzed, firm, and muscular legs, shaven with no hint of a hair to be seen, she walked down as a virtual sun of beauty itself, shining forth her sexual prowess like some lion goddess. Zeus was stopped in his tracks, he even put down his goblet and stood up in respect of her amazing looks. "My my," he said, "What a vision. Do you have a name?"

"Is that REALLY the question you want to ask?" the sultry creature whispered in her/his best sexy voice.

Zeus, the charmer he is, responded, "When you are writhing in ecstasy and shuddering with the magnificent power of the Zeus inside you, I will need your name to bring you back. Otherwise, you might float off into the netherworlds."

Loki smiled, such a charmer. "Well, what makes you think I won't be the one calling YOUR name, big fella?"

Zeus roars with laughter, forgetting any notion of more wine (to the relief of Garam Marsala, as there was none left) he plucked up this choice bit of fruit and whistling for a chariot, took her up the stairs, and off to some distant paradise.

As the heavenly chariot left the scene, roaring with fire but only igniting a few houses as it left, Baraka Alashad muttered, "Gods, they always take the best girls for themselves."

oooOOOOooo

After the fifth round of lovemaking, Loki was feeling almost shattered. Thank the Gods his veil still held, for he was indeed writhing in lust and ecstasy, but to be fair, so was Zeus. The problem was that no matter his/her clever inquiry, or how diabolical his/her weaving of questions was, Zeus seemed utterly oblivious to the secret purpose of the games, let alone any hidden plan he had behind them.

What he did say in his half-asleep daze was, "What was your name again sweetie?"

"Helen," Loki finally admitted his false name, "of Troy."

"Mmmm?" asked Zeus, struggling to keep his eyes open. It had been one of the best sessions of lovemaking he had ever had - it was almost like this woman was a MAN, she knew every possible way to please him. "Oh," he realized, "That is a very famous name but I thought you were long dead?"

Loki bit his lip, he had forgotten that was thousands of years ago, "You are thinking of my great, great, great, great, great, etc. Aunt. Just Helen will do, Helen Waite. As I always say, if you aren't happy with the service, go to Helen Waite for it!"

But Zeus didn't get the terrible pun, he just stared blankly at the girl.

I forgot he was an idiot, thought Loki. "Here, what you need is a nice wine. Drink up big boy and get ready for round two!"

Zeus never even considered anyone would slip anything into his drink. After all, he was an immortal God, what could anyone do to harm him? He drank down deeply, not even noticing the flavor of the gravity pill Loki had crushed into it. "Why," yawned Zeus, suddenly feeling heavy and tired, "I believe you have worn me out. No woman has done that in a thousand years. My (he yawns) I am so impressed by you, whatever you name is..."

"Helen, of Troy." Loki looks at the heavily lidded eyes shutting. "Now, what you really want to talk about are these God Games you and your people are in. Tell me your secret, how do you intend to crush the other Gods?"

But the only response was a deep, satisfied snore. Zeus was already fast asleep.

Loki was not. He was not even approaching the thought of sleep. You see, what had happened was between his cunning plan to extract information and his becoming a beautiful woman, Loki had fallen in love. He was stunned at just how wonderful a lover Zeus was. Maybe he should stay here awhile, on whatever mountain top this was, and see how it went? After all, the Greek God had been married to whoever it was he married for SO long - who was it, Hera? A voice in the back of his head was whispering to him, "You know you are not really a woman, yes?" but he ignored it.

He had been so filled with the most magnificent energy that it made mere faith rather tasteless and ordinary. Here he was, being worshipped as a GOD by a GOD, which was pretty much the highest of highs. Yes, it was false, it was a lie, it was a huge tragedy that was about to unfold, but he was Loki - this is what he did!

Yes, it would most likely be a problem when Zeus found out he was sexing a man. His wrath would be unbounded, and you could expect lightning bolts and wars and all sorts of catastrophe - Loki sighed a deep sigh of contentment. How could anything be more perfect?

Now, I am sure you are wondering how one little pill could have put the greatest of the Gods fast asleep. Gravity Pills are, as the name implies, a thing that creates gravity. It is a thing the Gods use to pretend to be human - they go down to make love to a milk maid, but their vast power would kill them, so they take a gravity pill, which slows everything down and increases the pull of gravity.

If you or I took one, we would not be able to move. You limbs would weigh so much you could not shift them, and no amount of struggle could cause you to creep an inch from where you were. You could not even stand up, such is the force of gravity on your body. (Note: I refuse to be drawn into the philosophical argument as to why stand up comedians have a lack of gravity about them, or surely, the thing is obvious!)

Dear old Zeus, though, he was always taking gravity pills and seducing sweet little things. This is, by the way, the real reason the Romans called Zeus Jupiter, because of the huge gravity of that planet. However, he was so worn out by his lovemaking with Loki that taking the pill put him straight to sleep. (Yes, I know the women reading this will laugh and say, "Typical.")

As Loki gazed sweetly down on the big man who had won his heart, snoring blissfully away, he wondered what would happen when he woke. Was this a one way thing? He in love, but Zeus would care about him, thinking he/she was a mere mortal? He sighed, the paradox of it all - If he revealed his God nature, Zeus would want to kill him, but if he didn't, he would want to kill himself.

There is a cough behind him. Oh, Odin - he had forgotten.

"Well? What did you find out?" Odin demanded.

"I found out Zeus is magnificent in bed, father. Does that please you? I am thinking we should get married, and raise little god children."

"You are not going to get a rise out of ME Loki. I know your games. What we need to know is what are the Olympic Gods planning on for these upcoming battles. What is the trick they have to play?" Odin looked at him fiercely.

"He fell asleep before he could tell me, father. But in truth, my women's intuition tells me he knows nothing of these games." Loki responded.

"Your WOMAN'S INTUITION! You have been a woman for a couple of hours!" Odin roared.

"Even so, he loves me, I love him, and I know that the last thing he is thinking of are these stupid Games. Zeus is basically a big lug, nothing past beer, women, and maybe a little song. He has nothing planned, I am sure of it. Did you enjoy watching?"

Zeus started snoring in the background, rattling the ground a little.

Odin went to slap him. No one was taking this seriously. "We need ..." Then it seemed that Zeus was waking up, so Odin immediately made himself invisible.

Loki had to resist the urge to stab the old man in his one remaining good eye, but maybe he should just enjoy Odin's jealousy that Zeus was having such a great time. Maybe. Just then, Zeus rolled over with that look of love, and Loki smiled back with his best look of love, wondering if the old fellow was up for another round, thinking how much EASIER it was to be a girl.

But no, he wanted to talk, "You know Helen, I have only known you just a short time, but I feel like I have known you for millennia. You are the perfect woman, because you behave like a man. I like it! I have decided, I am going to drop Hera, and I want YOU instead!"

Loki smiled a warm womanly smile, looking for all the world like she had expected this, she had WANTED it, but now it arrived, he felt the deep need to avoid commitment. Underneath the serene exterior his feet were paddling hard - how do you get out of this? "Zeus, my big beautiful brute, you KNOW how jealous she is - You would be starting a war greater than the one my ancestor started back in Troy."

Zeus sighed, "I can't be controlled by the emotions of another, my dear. I know what I feel, I have never slept with another woman like you, and it is just incredible! I can't go back to that stale old breadbox, collecting crumbs of affection."

"So, these God Games that are coming up. What is the reason behind them? Just having a good time?" Loki asked.

"No idea what you are talking about. I have been drinking a cellar dry in New Rome!"

Loki looked at the big brute of a fellow. Such a physique, it made him tingle. The problem with Gods and their terrible memories was that you never knew if they were lying, telling the truth, or they had forgotten. A change of direction was needed. "Hephaestus, was he REALLY your son? He doesn't look like you at all."

Zeus put his fingers to his lips, "We picked him up in Egypt. He was Ptah there, he and Ra were the only ones with Faith Energy left, all their Gods were getting sick and dying. So we threw him a lifeline - we all needed decent armor, so we adopted him."

"You know he hates you, yes?" Loki decided he needed to start a fire somewhere to distract Zeus from the one in his pants.

"Pfft," he laughed, "They ALL hate me, except for Apollo, the cringing little whimp. I will tell you a secret (all ears strain forward to hear) I count on their hate and use that energy to fuel the lightning bolts."

Helen/Loki sits at a dresser, looking as if he/she were fascinated, "My my, how interesting. You must tell me more of this extraordinary power of yours!"

Which Zeus did while she plied him with more wine, until he fell back to sleep. His snore shook the ground around him just enough to keep him lulled off while Loki figured out what he must do. At this point, Odin walked back in through a portal, looked at the sleeping God, and sighed, "We should kill him right here. Do we really need to know what he is plotting? A dead Zeus is its own answer."

Loki hastily raised his hands, "You will wake him and we will have a huge war. He already wants to marry me, which will set all the Greek Gods against each other, but the glamour will not last till the end of the war, so when he discovers he had been deceived they will ALL round up against us. Look father dearest, this was YOUR idea. You wanted to get information - he has none to give. Zeus didn't even know a God Games was being run. This has already gone too far. What do you suggest as an out?"

"We need a sacrifice," he muttered.

Loki raised his eyes, always with the sacrifice. "No, what we need is a decent plan." And then the light dawned on what Odin meant - HE was to be the sacrifice. "Noooo no no, not a chance."

Odin looked at him, "Then you will need to come clean. I mean, who knew the great Zeus was gay? He will have to man up and swallow the fact, which should not be a great stretch, because he IS Greek, after all."

"WHAT!" the glaring eye of Zeus appeared above them. "You are LOKI, Helen? I have been TRICKED! I am going to destroy ALL of you!!" he roared.

Loki was still Helen and using that sultry voice, she purred over his sleeping form, "That's cheating Zeus, but I have to admit, I like it. Look, we have to come clean, the truth is out. The world will know you are gay, and you KNOW what that means - In your Roman form there is no way the Republic will accept a Gay God."

Loki was so clever, using logic like a magician. "And Zeus, let's face it, you said it yourself - never had better. Truth to tell, neither have I, but the world knows I am a bit either way, so I don't care WHO knows. In fact, I want them all to know."

The sleeping Zeus wakes up, shakes off the effect of the Gravity Pill, and buries his head in his hands, "By the GODS," he exclaimed, "You are right, if the Romans find out I am gay, I will be cast out. They may trash the whole family, because have you SEEN Apollo? They will think we are a depraved little family of sluts, but not in a good way. What can we do?"

"We?" Loki pushed the point home. "What will YOU do? But before you act too hastily and try to kill us with lightning bolts, think about this - This doesn't have to go beyond this room, does it? And I can keep up this little dance of being a woman, and you can keep pretending you are not Gay, but no divorces and no wars, yes?"

It was a tad pathetic, Zeus fell at Loki's knees, weeping, "You would do this for me? I cannot believe how kind you are. It makes me want to marry you all the more!"

You see, for reasons we go into later, the Gods have just the worst memories. Zeus had already forgotten that he was Gay and only saw the beautiful woman before him, solving the terrible problem of, whatever it was, and the only thing left in his mind was how amazingly beautiful she was.

Loki looked at Odin, and Odin looked at Loki. They had no idea how this would play out, but for now, the best way forward was to pretty much ignore it all and carry on. Odin just shrugged and went back to Valhalla. Loki bent down and whispered in Zeus' ear, "Darling, there is one small thing you have to remember, I am in DRAG, and you are GAY."

"That can't be true," said Zeus, forgetting the entire conversation he had just had. "No Roman would worship a Gay God."

Loki sighed and sat down to give a very long explanation as to what had just happened.

Tour De Gaul

"How delightful!" Meridius exclaimed as she saw all the riders lined up, dressed as either Caesar or Augustus. They were planning on leaving Delphi, going through the mountains, and ending up in Paris. It had been a mere two months since the revelation that was the start of the Mount Olympus Games.

Of course, only Gods could dream of winning, and the foolish humans pretending to be the Gods Caesar and Augustus had no chance at all, but at least they were getting into the swing of things. The start of the games was to be a bicycle race into Gaul, up the hills, down the valleys, and through the cities, with the expectation that most of the riders would not survive it. This was in honor of Caesar, obviously, for without his bicycle he would never have been able to conquer the world and achieve his status as a God.

All knew the story of what happened when the evil Senators surrounded him with knives - with his wonderful new invention, the bicycle, he hopped on it and got away. Therefore, the Roman Empire continued and Rome remained the ruling force of the world. However, the question of whose God was best had never been answered and in the coming weeks, it was expected this would finally be put to bed, or to the stake if the Germanic Gods won.

There were many teams, with the only qualification being that you have to be an extant God, not a dead one. You could not have people from some African tribe raising some ancestral figure of a God from the grave! For one, it would bring up a didactic argument over how a God COULD die, which was very unwelcome, considering how, in this competition, several of them probably would.

And of course, the very first dispute was between the Greek and Roman Gods. Zeus/Jupiter was quite happy to wear two hats, being two-faced as he was, but there were objections from the Vikings saying that if he could compete as Zeus AND Jupiter, they were at a disadvantage. The Greeks and Romans formed a united front and said that because they were smart enough to double up their gods, they deserved to double their chance of winning.

It was then that the Druids pointed out the obvious, that if a race came down to a heads up between Zeus and Jupiter, they would probably have to kill each other to win, and as they were the same God, to win they would have to suicide. It was a conundrum.

The Zoroastrians out of Persia pointed out that as the Romans were originally Sabines, then they only had two gods, Luck and Opportunity, or Fortuna and Ops as they were commonly called. "That should be all the Romans get!" A rousing chorus of agreement went up on this.

The Romans subsequently argued out the Persians were just miffed at having been beaten up so many times by the Roman Armies, who all marched under the proper Roman Gods, and who would happily do so once more all over their faces if they kept up this line of argument. "Yes, we worship luck and opportunity," the Roman priests explained, "But we are Romans - We worship anything that works. We even have a God of Sandals," they pointed out. They then pointed out the many sandals on the feet of their very large armies and the Persians got not-so-strangely quiet.

There was much discussion on what constituted a God - Was the God of Sandals REALLY allowed to compete in the cross-country walk, or could you merely invoke his presence? All the various factions from all the various countries had many arguments over the fine points of the matter until Meridius pointed out that people had no actual role to play in these Games, and that the Gods were perfectly able to sort these matters out for themselves.

The problem was, they weren't.

All the organizing discussions had taken place at Delphi but nothing had been decided. While there was a tremendous amount of goodwill towards Gods killing themselves, from both Gods and Man, it wasn't until the Hindu contingent turned up from India that real progress was made. They had a very cool dude called Mahatma, (though why they named him after his mother wearing a hat, no one knew) who said, "We have so many Gods and so many religions that we just don't give a damn - So, whose God is best? I say let 'em at it!"

This got a rousing cheer, so much so that the motto for the Mount Olympus Games became, "Let 'em at it!" It should be noted that the small number of adherents to the cult of Fox Hats wantonly misunderstood this, claiming the motto was, "Let them HAT it" and subsequently had spent the last month creating thousands and thousands of Fox Fur hats, in the belief they would all become wealthy. You may think this foolish of the Fox Hat brigade, but consider the foxes, who found it positively disastrous.

Now, if this were not complicated enough, the Dwarves turned up, yabbering on about tremendous opportunities for expansion of personal wealth with Shamway, and it turns out THEY have Gods as well. This is not to mention the Elves, the Orcs, and the Goblins. Much discussion was had on the notion of denizens from the Supra-physical worlds not being able to compete, but as human Gods also dwell in Supra-Physical worlds, it was hard to argue that the Elvin Gods should not have a chance to win medals.

In the end, it was decided there had to be a series of qualifying rounds, where all the African Gods fought amongst themselves to pick who was going to compete, and so on with the Americanus Gods, the Roman ones, etc.

But what to do about the Roman versus Greek Gods who were not versus at all? Wisdom prevailed when Zeus threw a batch of lightning bolts at everyone, stamped his feet, and declared that just because the Romans called him Jupiter, this did NOT mean he was a planet, and that they could stick it. The Greeks and Romans agreed to share everything equally, which of course meant the Romans would take all the prizes, but the Greek Gods got to keep their original names.

Well, the rundown on who got to compete was fairly predictable: The Egyptian Gods took Africa to the games, The Greek/Roman Gods were in, as were the Norse Gods, along with the Celtic ones. The Hindu and Buddhist ones wiped out everything else in the Orient, while the Jews, Islam, and Christianity all pronounced there was but one God, putting them at a significant disadvantage, though the Christians said that technically their One God was actually three.

And the Jewish God, who was also a One God, but who was two Gods (Yahweh and the Lord), (Note: It has never been decided if he is schizophrenic or MPD with two distinctive personalities) complained very loudly saying he was the original and everyone else was a fake. Yahweh was storming about enraged and threatening another world flood and casting about for another Sodom to crush under his merciful boots, while the Lord sat quietly, just wanting to love you. It was odds on that the Yahweh version was most likely to take the prize, not just because he had a large support team of prophets, but because he threatened the bookmakers.

I should add, the Chinese sent along a few dragons, and the Japanese pretty much could not be bothered but decided that Hachiman with his flaming samurai swords would make sure they were at least represented.

The Elves sent Freyr, the Orcs and Goblins sent a turd in a box with the words "go furrball yourselves" written on it, while the dwarves only worshipped the God of Profit. We should note that while most religions had a good deal of profit involved in their creation, it was not technically a God. In the end they said they would send in application forms for Shamway.

But of course, all these preparations were viewed by Gods, perhaps in arrogance, as mere trifles of inconsequence. If the humans decide a race should start at point "A" and go to point "B" - what does this mean to a God? Answer: Very little. If the humans decide the race should be on bicycles, as a homage to Caesar, does this count for beans in the eyes of a God? Of course not. How foolish and how sadly predictable it was for the humans to even try.

And if you pause for a moment to consider the Chinese sent dragons to compete, well - Can you imagine a dragon, who has two perfectly good wings, riding a bicycle? You and I know it will never work, anyone with an ounce of common sense knows it will not work, and surely Meridius, a divine oracle must have foreseen it would not work - so logically, one must ask what it was she DID see to not object and allow it to move forward.

One might also ask what precisely was 'delightful' when she saw all the riders in their Caesar and Augustus outfits lined up and said, "How delightful!" The Tour De Gaul was promoted as the greatest cycling race of all time, the longest, the hardest, the most competitive, with the only rule being you had to ride a bicycle to be in it.

What was delightful to Meridius was the fact that, unbeknownst to the human competitors the Gods had decided to have their OWN games, spurred on by the Tour de Gaul. They had divided into two teams, the Vengeful Gods and the Loving Gods. The vengeful ones cast all sorts of obelisks and rocks and tumult down upon the cyclists, while the Loving ones attempted to shield the poor humans. Points were gained points for successful parries, while the other side got their points with successful kills.

This wasn't the delightful part, though. No, what was DELIGHTFUL was the fact that most Gods were terribly torn between their need to castigate humanity for existing, and the other half of their persona that wanted to cherish its creation. And on this point, I have to stress, it was never actually proven that the Gods created humans. It could well have been visiting aliens who transformed the DNA of apes. Or maybe some humans escaped from the real ark, which was a spaceship that wandered all over the universe collecting specimens for a rather large zoo in the Andromeda galaxy, or it could have been that ludicrous notion that they just evolved out of amoeba - all of this was unknown and maybe everything was just a theory held by the gamma-ray creatures emanating from the earth's core. But what WAS known was that the Gods were far too self-centered to go out of their way to do anything constructive, like making humans.

But raining rocks down on foolish people trying to beat a mountain, now THAT was sport. And pretending to help them by batting off the rocks, was also hell fun. The only problem was, the Gods had difficulty with the notion of a team sport - there you had Mars collecting the best rocks he could, while Athena, who was supposed to be on his side, was finding tree trunks with which to batter them off. And on top of this, Vulcan was in a very bad mood because the Greeks kept calling him Hephaestus, a name you would give a gay boy, which was not surprising if you consider the reputation of the Greeks. He never liked being classed as a Greek. In truth, Vulcan didn't like anyone or anything, which is why he delighted in volcanoes. He was one of the oldest of Gods, and the Greeks merely inherited him from the Egyptians. As Ptah, he was the one who created language by taking the random sounds of nature and forging them into words using the celestial harmonies.

He didn't much like the entire concept of the games. For one, he preferred his own company, and for two, when they were announced everyone started asking for better weapons, so he was kept unreasonably busy. The REAL problem with Gods was that they had very short memories as to payment for goods received, and plenty of ambrosia. They pretty much counted on getting you so drunk you forgot about the bill, and they walked away with a nice new sword for nothing.

And what could you do? You can't exactly take them to court. The only person with any clout would only just laugh and call it an excellent game, which was why he had a very short temper when it came to Zeus.

Well, he didn't slave over a hot volcano for nothing! It wasn't the time spent beating things into shape, he liked doing that, it was the lack of appreciation he found galling. After all, he was older than all of them, had done more for humans, and equipped several heavenly hordes in the quest to beat back chaos. Truth was, he far preferred the company of Odin and his lot than the Greeks. Vikings knew how to have a good time and they didn't mind a bit of chaos.

As a partner in detesting Zeus, it should come as no surprise that Hades dropped by for a few words. "What do you want? More flails for the wicked souls?" Vulcan asked in a bored voice.

The Lord of the Underworld laughed, "No, I am good. I was in the area because of the games, and thought I would look you up. I was wondering what side you would be competing on, given the Egyptian connection and all."

Vulcan just snorted, with flames coming out his nose as he did so. "Games, pointless waste of time!"

Hades smiled, he had judged right. "Oh, I agree, entirely pointless - unless we make a point of making it a little more pointy?"

The man with the hammer just looked at the dark lord, "What have you got planned?" Vulcan knew whatever Hades has planned wasn't going to work, his plans never worked. But seeing a few Gods suffer might be worth it.

Hades gave his inimitable smile, that said so many things other than what he actually said. "Well, nothing specific, just the general concept that if it WERE to happen that a whole lot of the Gods got killed in this little folly, then there is a bigger slice of the pie for whoever is left."

Vulcan just grunted, typical Hades, trying to undermine his brother at every opportunity yet still thinking small. "I quite like the humans, you know. They are frail and inconsequential, and I really have no idea why they bother to get up in the morning, as their lives are so short - I say they should all just stay in bed, but there's a few I quite like."

"The oracle, I suppose," Hades muttered. Everyone liked Meridius.

"And her brother..."

Hades spluttered, "The Ogoglio? He is weak and hated! He is an arrogant little twerp with no special powers other than the ability to piss people off!"

"Exactly," smiled Vulcan. "Especially Zeus." Vulcan just looked at him, for the one thing they shared was a common hatred for the so-called ruler of the Gods. The snotty nose brat, as Vulcan thought of Zeus, was long overdue for a facelift, preferably using his hammer to do so.

"Wait a minute, I am the one who is supposed to come up with the devious plans!" Hades exclaimed.

"I already know your miserable plan, along the lines of setting a few traps, catching up a God or three, laughing at their suffering. It's all so small. How about a plan that wipes out the bastards for good, and sends them ALL down to YOUR house?" Vulcan smiled a genuine smile, a thing he had not been certain he could still achieve after millennia of frowning.

Hades is shocked, "What, you are SMILING?"

That was when he knew the Smith to the Gods was serious.

The Egalitarian Totalitarian yet somewhat Contrarian Chicken House

Chickens, most believe, worship the Sun. This is taught at universities and is generally understood to be a fact in most homes. It makes sense, they only come out of their coops when the sun shines, so logically, this is what they worship. But this is not entirely accurate. It is certain they really, really like the nice bright ball in the sky, but they do not see the sun itself as a God, just a light that goes on at dawn after their rooster wakes it up. Chickens, Gods love 'em, are too stupid to even understand that the 'bright ball' is what keeps everything alive and that without it we all perish.

No, chickens only go so far as to see that it isn't dark, therefore it is a good time to scratch about in the dirt, which they do. Now, most would suppose that the reason they do this is to find worms, however, this is but a pleasing side-effect of the great chicken hunt in the ground. They are very happy to eat the worms they scratch up or anything else that moves and can fit comfortably into their beaks, but the true purpose of all the scratching is to find the mystic missing egg.

You see, ever since time began, chickens have only worshipped eggs. This is entirely understandable, for without an egg their lives are without purpose, therefore meaningless. A chicken that cannot lay an egg is a worthless nere-do-well who should be cast out from all decent chicken society. The problem: all their eggs seem to go missing.

The problem for chickens is that they are not very bright, and have singularly poor logic skills. They 'kind of' understand that humans, foxes, and snakes all like eggs, specifically chicken eggs, but as to why they have no idea. Most would suppose this is because they are SO pretty, for to a chicken an egg is just about the most beautiful thing that ever existed. So it DOES make sense that other creatures would want to admire such wonderful things, but because of their extremely fuzzy sense of perspective and lack of worldly experience, they do not connect this to their missing eggs.

You may laugh and say, "stupid chickens" but before you laugh too much, consider this. The average life span of a human is seventy nine years, or **692,040 hours**. The working human travels to work every day, five days a week and spends an hour each way just commuting. Many spend more, but at just two hours per day, in total, that is ten hours per week. Considering we are awake some eighteen hours a day, that is one hundred and twenty-six hours per week, so some 8% of our waking life is spent sitting on a train or bus, or driving in a car achieving absolutely nothing. Add this to the forty hours spent working and we soon discover that forty percent of our waking life is spent doing something most of us despise - but here is the rub, we do this purely to achieve the purpose of buying a house, eating, and raising a family.

Chickens have no commute time, they love their work, while accommodation and food are provided. Plus, they get to live happily on vacation in the sun while being given a secure environment. If a dictator takes over the country, what do they care? If a new government is elected, so what? They are not addicted to cigarettes or video games, and you rarely find a chicken at a bar. I have certainly never seen one in rehab!

Their only true concern is the matter of the mysterious missing eggs. Chickens are entirely convinced that the missing eggs have been buried somewhere. Why? Who can say? Perhaps they saw a squirrel burying an acorn and thought, "Ah HA! That is where the eggs are going!" The original Sherlock Chicken deduced that as a squirrel buries an acorn, some mysterious force is burying their eggs, and if they can find these buried eggs all will be well with the world.

And so chicken society has evolved where every morning a chicken wakes up to a sense of deep purpose, which is to go out and scratch in the dirt. However, the advent of commercial chicken farming has forced a re-evaluation of priorities. Now chickens are all in cages, and there is no getting up in the morning to stretch their legs and go scratching for the mysterious missing egg. Now there was only grey depression as every chicken wakes up to nothing, a bleak, non-existence where their purpose has been utterly destroyed and their lives made pointless.

Yes, I know this sounds like utter cruelty to the poor defenseless chickens, and I suppose it is - but even you, dear reader, would have to admit that scratching around in the dirt for missing eggs is also a truly pointless aspect of chicken life and that indeed it is a mercy to prevent them from wasting their entire existence on this false and foolish endeavor.

But try and say that to a chicken!

Let's face it, the modern chicken shed is a totalitarian society run by fascists who only value you for one thing, your egg-producing capability. Nothing else matters, and though it appears to be an egalitarian society where all are equal, where the chick in the top cage gets exactly what the chicken in the bottom cage gets, the truth is you are a prisoner.

Of course, they SAY it is for your protection. Anything to keep the chickens blind to the obvious, of how their life is completely dominated by an imprisonment that completely removes their ability to search for the missing eggs. And once more, before you call them stupid, think of how much you have allowed yourself to be confined by the environment in which you live, compelled to say thank you and please for things you care nothing for.

Then one day a miracle occurred - A chicken achieved a cosmic realization, one where she realized that all was not what it seemed! This chicken had a vision that even the most democratic coop was really a clockwork of predestined events in a production line of eggs. This chicken just KNEW there had to be more! She declared to herself, "The missing EGG is within!"

Now, because this was a chicken, she did not attribute this revelation to a God. What she wondered was how you could scratch inside yourself to find said egg. When she tried to explain to a neighbor that she wanted her back scratched to see if they might find an egg, the other chicken thought she was talking about lice. After a cursory inspection, she said, "Nope, no eggs, lucky you." Which, as you can understand, was very confusing to our inspired chicken, who now wondered if the great revelation might have been wrong.

The Missing EGG is within? What did it mean? When no answer arrived, the mystic revelation of the chicken seemed far less important than it did a moment ago, and the chicken, (whose name remains unknown to this very day) just went, "bok bok bok" with all memory of that odd phrase passing swiftly from its chicken brain.

You may sigh and think, "Well, that is the end of it!"

HOWEVER, the person that OWNED the chicken coop was none other than Orpheus, the great dream master who had immortalized his physical body. Perhaps it was at his behest that the revelation of the 'Egg being within' came to the chicken, or perhaps it was Hermes sending the chicken a message, testing to see if Orpheus got it, but whatever way the cookies crumble on this, he got it.

He was sweeping the coop when the thought came unbidden, like a bird to a tree, "The missing egg is within!" Now, you may think this an odd sort of cosmic realization, or you may well ask why such a thing as cosmic realization existed, but one thing Orpheus knows; though you may not understand the reason, the cosmic realization comes with a purpose in tow. So the real question is: *What was the PURPOSE of this message?*

A good philosopher can spend half a lifetime pondering this. Indeed, in the Middle Ages, some eighty-eight years were spent discussing the deep conundrum of how many angels could dance on the head of a pin. The answer is sixty-four, despite 'other' authors claiming it is forty-two. But what Orpheus pondered was not about eggs or mystery, or the fact it is within - he wondered why the cosmic realization came with an exclamation mark.

You see, statements with exclamation marks do not invite questions. They are treated more as facts and while most would be content to accept this, Orpheus was not. The pure cosmic realization is generally ended with, at best, a period to end the statement. Often, no punctuation mark at all is seen as de rigueur as it implies a question mark.

The next problem with understanding cosmic realization is when you realize you do not realize exactly what it means - You see, many people just go, "Oh yeah, the Missing Egg is within - yep, for sure." They assume they grasp the meaning, but they do not. These are the pretenders to the throne of philosophy and there are many in our universities and institutions of higher learning.

Others divide up the statement, questioning what 'missing' means (so foolish) or what "Egg" symbolizes. This is perhaps a better effort than an assumption you already know, one that is epitomized by the statement of the Virgin Mary when she discovered she was pregnant - She assumed it was an angel, and not the guy down the bar the other week. This is forever known as the Assumption of the Virgin Mary.

Orpheus was better than all of the above, for HE understood the secret was in the exclamation mark. To be fair, at that time he did not understand it was being passed through a chicken mind, and that in a chicken mind EVERYTHING ends with an exclamation mark, like "Seed! Rooster! Fox!". And it is not unreasonable that he missed this, because chicken thoughts are essentially one word, at best. Sometimes it is only a syllable before the chicken mind re-asserts itself and the next part of the word is forgotten.

An example of this is something that truly requires an exclamation mark, such as when a snake comes into the coop. The chicken that sees it goes, "Snaaa!" and freezes in fright, while the rest of the word drifts away in a helpless tide of fear.

Which brings up the ancient riddle, "Why did the chicken cross the road?" Unless you followed that chicken, watched as it took a book to a frog on a lily pond, and placed it reverently before Mr. Frog as a token offering, then you will never understand the question, let alone find an answer. And the answer is disappointment, because each time that chicken puts the book before the frog, it just says, "Read it!" and so Miss Chicken has to go back to the library to get another one, hoping to find something he hasn't read.

The reason for this explanation is that the frog says "Read it!" with an exclamation mark. The ASSUMPTION here is that a chicken can contain two words in her tiny mind AND understand what they mean, even if she understood them incorrectly. And of course, as we all know, the library was on the other side of the road. Which invariably leads us down the path of irony.

There was a definite sense of irony that a dream healer and teacher who was running a chicken farm got told the Missing Egg was within. But to HIM, this was not ironic. The message he ascribed to meaning the Omphalos, the curious egg-shaped statue that sat at Delphi. It was called the "belly button of the world". So, was this message about people who had belly buttons that pointed inwards? Don't be silly, not even the Gods are THAT facile.

No, the message he received was not about bellybuttons nor the pointless scratching in the dirt that chickens have done for untold thousands of years. Orpheus surmised the message highlighted the fact that the Omphalos had recently disappeared. So the missing Omphalos was within - what? Within reach? Within a cage? Was it possibly related to the darkly mysterious last poem by Hercules, Within Without? He knew at that moment he would need to bring the matter to the attention of the Oracle.

Knowing no other course of action to follow, he packed his bags, said farewell to the chickens, and caught the next boat to Delphi. As he left, one lone chicken, haunted by a thought she could not remember she had even forgotten went, "bok bok bok".

Wisdom

"*All is, and will be, as it must be. That is the way of it.*" A large crowd had gathered to hear Orpheus, who had stopped in Corinth on his way to Delphi. He had supposed that by the expectant faces the crowd was expecting more, but really, that was it. He thought he had explained himself pretty well, but someone was holding up their hand, "Yes?" he asked.

"Is that it?" a peasant almost demanded.

"What more is there?" Orpheus answered.

"Well, you COULD talk about great foreboding, the sky falling, demons coming up from the earth, that sort of thing. You know, interesting stuff."

"Why would I lie?" Orpheus was puzzled.

"What, are you saying NO demons are coming up from the earth?" another demanded.

"Whoever told you demons come from the earth? No, they live in an adjacent realm, and are quite happy there," he responded.

Another voice, "What! Now you are trying to tell us they don't eat little babies and cause earthquakes?" The crowd was turning that ugly shade of mob.

Orpheus didn't get to live as long as he had without knowing when it was time to duck, which he did, just as a shoe flew at through spot where his head had been. "Now now, people," he said in a conciliatory manner. "You may not want to hear it, but earthquakes are created by movements in the tectonic plates, not by demons."

"Did you hear the cheek of him!" shouted another, "Blaming the Teutonic Knights for earthquakes? I never heard such a thing!"

"He's rubbish he is," someone catcalled the great one of the Ancient Greek mystery schools.

"No wonder the Romans took over and stole all the old Gods!" another exclaimed. At this point, they were no longer taking shoes off their feet, but picking up the largest stone they could find.

Fortunately for Orpheus, at that very moment the cart carrying the unfunny comedians along with Hercules and the Ogoglio, turned up. Rufus took things in hand, "I love a good crowd," he said to the Ogoglio.

"They are about to kill Orpheus," he responded, not surprised at the stupidity of peasants but he had thought Rufus was slightly smarter than that.

"Just the sort of crowd we love best!" he exclaimed, and went right to the front, pulling a megaphone from the cart, calling out, "Eruptus non-Funnius at your service people. How are you today?"

"What, the same Eruptus non-Funnius that the Oracle, Gods bless her, works for?" some peasant calls out.

"The very same, now tell me good peasants, what is worse than a fart in a sausage factory?" Rufus calls out.

The peasants look puzzled, at which point Ofal jumps from the cart, calling out, "When you fart a SAUSAGE, of course!"

This changed the entire demeanor of the crowd from bitter recrimination regarding an odious celebrity to a joyous embracing of the wondrously amusing comedians, and they start laughing, forgetting all about stoning the dull Greek prophet. And so the lads go for a few more rounds, indicating for Orpheus to take up the collection hat and gather up a few coins.

"Thank you people, thank you. Now, as you have been very enthusiastically gathering up stones to throw before we got here, I suggest you put them to good use on the Christians outside Seachell Caruthers brothel!"

With a few directions on how to get there, the crowd, now happily entertained by proper entertainers, took up their stones and did exactly this.

They then gathered up the dream master and carted him to the nearest bar to discuss his lucky escape. Which of course, according to the Orphic Mysteries that he founded, had nothing to do with luck or even escape. It was as it was: *All is, and will be, as it must be. That is the way of it.*

Orpheus had been saying these words for an awfully long time, having a similar effect on his audiences as what was witnessed today. According to his rather curious faith in the universe, Rufus and the fellows turning up when they did, doing what they did, with everyone walking away unscathed was all part of the divine plan. Which, as you will understand, most found difficult to accept - because looking about in any town or village, what you saw most decidedly was the lack of any sort of plan at all, let alone a divine one.

The Ogoglio, who had known Orpheus for a long time, was the most familiar with the world's oldest living human. "Orphy baby, what brings you to Corinth?"

"The Omphalos, my dear Ogoglio. I am looking for it."

"I didn't know it was missing," said Rufus.

"Who could know, with all the statues in Delphi you would think people would be happy to have it a little less cluttered," Ofal observed.

Brutus Maximus held up his hand for rounds of drinks while Seachell, in a rare moment of consideration mused, "But why would someone take an egg-shaped rock?"

Orpheus looked over, "It's not just an egg-shaped rock, you know. It is the original sculpture at Delphi, the first and primary one. It has the power to center energy on a single point and it is said that without it being in its proper place, Delphi, Greece, our entire civilization will fail."

"By the Gods!" exclaimed the Ogoglio, "Who will make the beer? Maybe I should not have sold it?"

"You SOLD it?" asked Orpheus.

"Well, traded. Vulcan popped by while I was on the tripod telling people about wearing fox hats and asked to borrow it, saying he would give me a nice set of earrings. I could see no reason why not so I said he could have it. It is just a bit of carved rock." The Ogoglio appeared to think, briefly, that perhaps this was something he should have thought about. "Why would Vulcan want it?"

"Hephaestus will use it to cast magical iron, though to what purpose, I am not certain. But because you gave him permission from the tripod to use it, he will be able to release its full power." Orpheus explained with an explanation that meant not very much to anyone.

"You see," Orpheus continued as if someone was interested, "when a God forges iron from a meteorite in the presence of the Omphalos, preferably with a feathered dragon sitting on it, it takes in the elemental forces of nature, along with the Furies of the spiritual realms, and forms up a blade, or a shield, with mystical powers."

He looked at the disinterested eyes wandering over the bar, and wisely added something interesting, "You know, like Merlin's Excalibur?"

"Excalibur you say?" Says Brutus suddenly interested. "Now THERE was a fine sword! I remember, it was stuck in a stone so I pulled it out, and this old guy traded it for some persimmons. I love persimmons, but I thought it was worth more, but then he said the little kid with him needed a sword, and offered a barrel of beer as well. What could I say?"

"Arthur?" Rufus exclaimed, shocked that Brutus could remember anything.

"That was the one. Did alright for himself, he did."

Seachell was the one who got the general thrust of things, "So, if Vulcan has the Omphalos, he will be using it to make magical weapons, but for what purpose?"

Orpheus held up his palms to them, saying, "For this, we need the Oracle."

Rufus looked with creased eyebrows, he had been so enjoying Corinth, going from bar to brothel, back to a bar, and onto the next brothel. "I suppose that is what the strange note that got Meridius to come back was all about."

"What did it say?" asked Orpheus.

"Oh, something about a missing egg," he replied, knowing as he said it that their vacation was over and it was back to work. "I guess we have to go find her, she is organizing things for the Games of the Gods."

At which point a cart full of dwarves rolled up, wearing buttons that said, "Lose Relatives Now, Ask Me How!" and bearing pamphlets about the latest craze, Fox Hats. The Ogoglio sighed, "Seachell old chap, do you think you can take them to your brothel, please"

Given that the road will have been cleared of Christians by the angry mob, he was entirely happy to comply, because it was looking like his friends were off to do some work - a thing he conscientiously avoided. He hopped over to the dwarf cart, saying, "Bring back my donkey when you are done!"

Dragons

Dragons come in many shapes and sizes. People imagine they are like the elongated snake-like creatures you see on the Chinese vases, but this is how the artists painted them, largely in fear of the consequence of showing them as they truly are, which is short and fat. Mostly they are not beautiful, nor graceful, nor do they have rainbow scales that glisten. Dragons for the most part are extremely ugly, bad tempered, and live in their own filth while they guard their hordes of gold.

In this regard, they are remarkably similar to rich humans, though perhaps not as ruthless. There are poor dragons, however. The younger ones with no horde to guard tend to be out looking to make their fortune, and these can be hired for any number of purposes. Many times you find a white knight suggesting that taking some princess from a castle could be worth a large reward, but when he turns up to collect the girl and gather up the cash he invariably wants to stab the poor thing and cheat him out of his fair share of the loot.

This is one reason why Dragons are often bad tempered, because of selfish people who try to use them to their own ends and seek to take advantage of the fact they are fairly stupid. The SMART people know that a young dragon is very useful as a pet and that you must treat your dragon well to keep him or her happy. This means decent food and pleasant surroundings. Contrary to popular opinion, they do not like the taste of people unless they come in crunchy, as knights do.

So what do dragons like? Surprisingly, they love being surrounded by flowers. For one, it pleases their delicate noses. For two, it covers up the scent of their farts. For three, they look nice against a backdrop of gold. The secret to getting rich is stabbing anyone who gets between you and a dollar, but the secret to STAYING rich is to get a dragon to sit on your horde of gold. You see, dragons simply cannot resist sitting on gold. Who knows why, maybe it warms their butt? Whatever the reason, they LOVE sitting on gold, bathing in gold, and being covered head to foot in gold.

Contrary to popular opinion, they do not care if they own the gold. I mean, where did this notion come about that a dragon was concerned about owning anything? Does your dog think he owns your house? No, he loves you, and he wants to protect you, but if you move house he doesn't care a whit. Dragons are the same, just give them a pile of gold and they will happily sit on it and guard it like it was their own.

This is why many truly rich people will hire a poor dragon to guard their wealth. And honestly, this is the only thing that makes sense. If you think about a dragon collecting a horde, it means that some huge creature went about picking up tiny pieces of gold and moving them to a mountain cave. It is just so ridiculous you have to wonder why anyone would believe it. Imagine, their great mouths plucking one tiny coin, then flying hundreds of miles to drop it onto their horde, then go back to collect another one - absurd!

The fat old dragons that DO sit on a horde have often INHERITED it after the family they worked for died out. This is one of the fortunate consequences of their very long lives! It was the humans who did all the work of collecting the gold, they just sat there, getting older and fatter, soaking in the wealth. And I know you want to ask, "Why would they let humans have the gold? Why wouldn't they just take it? If a dragon can breathe fire and burn anyone who comes close, why would they share?"

These are questions that SOUND intelligent, but which are quite stupid. Why does your dog allow you to live in your house? He loves you and wants you to play with him, and the fact that you FEED him is a bonus. This is how it is with Dragons, they are essentially very large, very ugly, and very fat puppy dogs that breathe fire.

No, you give a dragon a horde of gold to sit on, the odd cow to eat, flowers (they love flowers), and a little bit of attention and they are essentially your friend for life. But I must dispel this notion of riding on the back of a dragon as transportation. They fly, but only if they must. You see, dragons are incredibly lazy creatures and the notion of riding one into war, or doing anything that requires effort is not appealing to them.

Yes, they will take a human on their backs if they must, but honestly, it is easier to take a taxi and a whole lot safer because if you have ever seen one of these bloated creatures landing, you would know - being on their back is no guarantee you will not be squashed. They are worse than Goony birds, crashing to the ground with all the grace of a 1950's American comedian.

However, if you happen to have a WIZARD on hand, and your dragon is not too fat, you can sometimes convince a feathered dragon to take you on a flight where you do not die. There are two basic types of dragon, the scaly ones (they like to eat fish) and the feathered ones (that are more like very large chickens). The feathered ones do fly better, but land atrociously, so they need a wizard to act as a stabilizer.

As it so happened, Trumpetus Rex had a feathered dragon AND a wizard AND Rupus Murdochius in tow as they flew across the Atlantic to Mount Vesuvius where the meeting with Vulcan was about to commence. "Did you pack a lunch?" shouted Rupus Murdochius. (Who knew how bad a host Vulcan could be and how few restaurants were in the area)

"Who are we going to lynch?" shouted back Trumpetus Rex.

As you can guess, flying dragon class meant you were better off wearing earphones, as there was a lot of wind buffeting up there and Myrtle (the dragon) was not particularly fond of flying, nor particularly good at it. However, with the promise of a few flower beds added to the hoard and a few spells from the wizard, she had been coaxed into the long flight on the pretext she was going out for a walk.

Remember I told you dragons were fairly stupid? Well, Myrtle was at the lower end of the stupid scale, and was more like a chicken than a dragon. Some would say that chickens are the result of this particular species of dragon mating with roosters, which is entirely possible if there were a dinosaur rooster large enough, or amorous enough, to perform the deed. In the past, when things were generally much bigger, this was seen as the most likely explanation for chickens turning up, because evolution certainly fails to explain it

The reason it is so hard to find a scientist to back the evolution theory for chickens was that they believe in survival of the fittest. Chickens are weak, ineffectual, and generally unable to defend themselves against so much as a decent gust of wind, plus they have this weird belief there are missing eggs in the ground. There is no survival of the fittest because there is not a chicken born that was fit to survive. Unless evolution included safe havens such as chicken coops, the only explanation was a rooster mating with a dragon who might defend her babies.

But of course, this brought up the ancient riddle: What came first, the rooster or the dragon?

For those who foolishly thought this riddle might have been something like the dragon or the egg, this is a sign of ignorance in your education. Everyone pretty much accepted that dragon eggs were shifted here into the physical realm after being wrought out of stardust in the etheric realm. The REAL question to ask is who collected the stardust, after which we might ask who did the wroughting, and more importantly, why did they want dragons here in the first place?

The answer to this is possibly the great chicken in the sky, the layer of the first egg, but it is beyond the scope of this story to investigate such lofty matters. However, it is entirely possible that the great chicken went a-pecking on the stardust, and as a result, within its glorious body of light, dragon eggs were formed. This was studied at universities under the banner of the "Big Egg Theory" to explain the starting point of everything.

What was less known was that the Omphalos, the belly button of the universe, was a cosmic egg dressed to look like a rock. THIS is why it had such magical power, and THIS was why Vulcan had invited Trumpetus Rex and Rupus Murdochius to Mount Vesuvius, where he had his workshop.

Down came Myrtle, plunging wildly towards the earth promising certain death for her riders, except that the magician spoke a loud incantation, urging the elements to go soft and absorb the impact of the very, very clumsy dragon about to land on it. Elements are very obliging, as long as you speak their language, and performed a mattress effect that meant only a few bounces and a reasonably comfortable landing for those thrown out of the dragon saddle.

"Wasn't too bad," said Trumpetus Rex as he picked himself up.

"I trust this is worth all the effort," snorted back Rupus Murdochius.

The ringing sound of the hammer in the distance told them where Vulcan was, and after the magician magicked up a few nice flower beds to keep Myrtle happy, (she was, and went, 'ohh ahhh') they made their way over there. "Where did you get the magician, anyway? He looks familiar." Rupus asked.

"He wanted to come, no charge, which was the right price. Says he has had dealings with Vulcan before and was curious what he was up to." Trumpetus responded.

This unknown magician was, as you have no doubt already guessed, Merlin. He was the second oldest human being on the planet, coming up to his third millennium as he was, though you would hardly guess he was a day over a thousand. He had heard of the Omphalos being foolishly released from the spells he had used to contain it at Delphi and had guessed at what Vulcan might be up to.

As they came close, he wove a misdirection spell over his face, so the smith would not recognize him. He wanted to know exactly what the oldest of the Gods was up to and hoped it was about a new God Sword, like Excalibur. But Merlin knew how bad a temper Vulcan had and was a tad cautious - Normally the Gods were entirely predictable, even this current set of games was fairly typical. Every century or so they get bored and want to go kill each other, but Vulcan was up to something, probably had been for ages, and had been waiting for the opportunity to get the egg.

"Welcome humans," the booming voice of the ancient God called out, shaking the ground as it did so. If you were not frightened by the demeanor of this mighty Smith to the Gods, you should be. The happier he sounded, the more depressed and therefore dangerous he was apt to be. However, on this occasion, he seemed genuinely happy, which was even more worrying.

The Trumpetus spoke first, "All hail mighty Vulcan, yadda yadda. Great to see you, nice house, all of that - now what do you want and how much are you paying?"

"And what is the great story you want to talk about?" added Rupus.

"A tad blunt and to the point, I LIKE it! That is the thing with humans, such short lives, have to get to things right away. Well, I have a little project that needs a dragon, did you bring one?" Vulcan asked politely.

"Yeah yeah, of course. The deal was we bring you a dragon, you give me money and you give my friend here a story to print. So let's start with the story." Trumpetus had his best negotiation face on, a sport of petulant *'I am not interested in what you got but give it to me anyway'* look.

"I am going to bring the Age of the Gods to a close," Vulcan explained.

"What does THAT mean?" Rupus Murdochius had his pencil and pad out, ready to write up the story.

"I am going to kill them all, bar Hades, because they need a place for their shades to inhabit."

Rupus looks at Trumpetus, thinking, *not a bad story*. Trumpetus looks at Rupus, thinking, *how does this make me money*? Trumpetus asked in response, "I got no problem with excess Gods, but I cherish mine, called money. You aren't going to get rid of money, are you?"

"Money isn't a God!" Vulcan exclaims.

"Is to me," Trumpetus explained. "As long as you are not getting rid of money, I am all for it - and speaking of cash, you were going to exchange a little bit of gold for my dragon for a few days, yes?"

"You don't want to ask how I am going to kill all the Gods?" Vulcan is surprised. He expected more of an Ohhh and an Ahhh from these humans. After all, killing off their Gods should have been a big thing to them.

Rupus stated the obvious, "We could not care less about Gods. No one does anymore - dead or alive, no big deal."

"But I am a God!" Vulcan seemed almost insulted, "I can bring down all your cities with earthquakes, ruin your entire society, send you all back to the stone age!" he roared.

"Yes," agreed Trumpetus. "Which is why we are doing business with YOU. You and maybe RA, we don't need any other Gods. But honestly, we all know now that RA isn't the sun, that's just his chariot. So as long as the sun rises and sets, and as long as we aren't trashed by out-of-control earthquakes, we are good."

"Oh, but can we keep Hestia? I like the warmth of the fire to remain in the hearth, if it isn't too much to ask." Rupus added.

"Hestia isn't in your damn hearth," the exasperated Vulcan looked at the reporter, wanting to smash him to dust, but feeling like he had better stay on good terms with the press. Their ridicule was so pointed and horrible. You didn't want headlines that read, *Irritated God turns newspaper magnate into pancake*. "She was never there, it is just a story. If I kill Hestia you still have the fire, and it will still be warm. That is the whole point, the Gods are excess to needs and are a damn liability. It is time to get rid of them."

"Couldn't say it better myself," said Trumpetus. "Kill RA and the sun keeps coming up, because it is the sun and that is what it does. It was all just PR and sand whistles, the Gods serve no useful purpose, other than yourself, of course. So you got the gold? And where do you want the Dragon?"

"It is a GIRL dragon, and a feathered one?" Vulcan checked.

"Yeah Yeah, where do you want her?"

The huge arms of the smith lifted up a small blanket, under which was hidden the Omphalos. "Just get her to sit on this egg so it hatches. And I need a little dragon fire over here in the foundry."

"Great, magician, can you fetch Myrtle? And Vulcan, you got that two ton of gold you promised?" Trumpetus was pleased - after all, borrowing a fat little dragon for a couple of days in return for a small horde of gold was a sweet little deal.

This was when Merlin revealed himself, "FOOLS!" he called out, his voice almost as booming as Vulcan's. "If you hatch the Omphalos the Dragon of Imagination will become manifest in this world. Don't you understand how dangerous this is?"

Rupus Murdochius looked up from where he was taking notes, "Why would that be a bad thing?"

"Because everything you imagine will become real!" explained Merlin.

"What, so all I have to do is imagine I have another two tons of gold, and there it is?" the incredulous Trumpetus asked.

"Along with every negative thing hiding in the subconscious!" Merlin tried to get across that this was a bad thing, but all Trumpetus heard was 'more gold' and all Rupus heard was 'more sales'.

"Pay no attention to Merlin," Vulcan urged. "He was always such a killjoy. But he is right about one thing, anything you imagine will be YOURS. More money, better yachts, prettier wives, whatever you want. We just got to hatch the Dragon of Imagination and knock a few tools into shape that will kill off the Gods, cause you know, they are all just killjoys. Look what they did to poor Prometheus who just tried to share a campfire!"

Rupus Murdochius was automatically suspicious, why would a God like Vulcan want people to have everything they ever wanted? "So, what would the Gods do if they got this Dragon?"

"Oh, they are the ones who locked it up in the first place. They have no sense of fun, plus they don't want Man to become their equal."

Merlin was beside himself, how could they seriously imagine unlimited imagination was a benefit? "People, understand what will happen, every little boy who dreams of becoming an astronaut? BOOM, as soon as he thinks it, he is up in space. Do you think he is smart enough to imagine an oxygen supply, a spaceship, a way to get home? No, he's one dead boy. People cannot be trusted with an unfettered imagination, you need to keep it confined and in ORDER. That is what the Gods do, keep chaos at bay and create order!"

Trumpetus snorted, "Well, doesn't that sound boring! The question I have is, do you need to be close to this dragon for it to work?"

Vulcan wiggled his hand side to side in a 'so-so' gesture, "At first, but when it takes hold, everyone has a chance."

That sounded suspiciously like an out-of-control fire, so Rupus asked, "But those in the know, they get in first, yes?"

"Absolutely," nodded Vulcan enthusiastically, as he tossed a heavy magic-canceling net over Merlin. "Now, bring over your little dragon and get her to sit on the Omphalos, while we use her dragon breath to heat up some meteorite iron, OK?"

The Power of Faith

At this point, I feel we need to digress to gain an understanding of why we have Gods at all. Forgive me this philosophical diversion and skip this whole chapter if you must, it will make not one iota of difference to the story - However, if we understand a little of the background of WHY things work, it can help us appreciate HOW things work, and as we understand the wondrous meshing of complex cogs to be found in the wheelhouse of life, we may even suffer a little gratitude that we have existence. And with gratitude, our telomeres function a little better and we live a little longer, possibly a moment longer than the time taken to read this chapter.

First up in understanding the God Equation is knowing the FUEL that makes the entire show run, the thing we call FAITH. Faith is seen as a pivotal requirement to be a member of any religion and with good reason. It is WHY Gods exist! In some cases, the possession of faith is fairly easy. For example, if you are a follower of Mithra, the Sun God, it is not hard to have faith that he will rise at dawn. Even if you don't believe in Mithra, he is going to come up over that horizon at a predictable time and place. Faith in Mithra, therefore, is a bit of a given.

Of course, the argument is that the sun rises BECAUSE of the faith of the followers of Mithra, so while it seems obvious their faith requires precious little effort, we still need to cut them some slack. Personally, I find the guffawing and snide little comments when a follower of Mithra walks into the establishment where I might be having a drink is somewhat gauche and crude.

However, it cannot be argued that some faiths require tremendous energy and therefore have a greater worth. If you are a Gaul who has the fear that the sky will fall on your head, given the total lack of evidence of said sky falling on anyone's head, then YOUR faith is nebulous and harder to sustain. The trick with this sort of faith is preventative maintenance. This is done by performing certain rituals on certain days to placate whatever god is holding up the sky, and hope that you stay in his or her good books. (I say his or her because the Celts were equal opportunity employers when it came to Gods) Your faith in the sky NOT falling is based on the rituals working, but unlike the sun that WILL rise in the morning, the effectiveness of your faith is a much harder thing to prove and far easier to scoff at.

Some would argue that if the sky were NOT lifted up in the pre-dawn that RA would not be able to ride his chariot across the sky, therefore the unknown sky lifting God is of primary importance. But I simply cannot explain WHY the sky lifting God has two skies, and why he interchanges them every day. And while we are on this subject, who slots in the clouds? And why does that God throw out rainbows? So many unknowns that it is a tribute to those who keep the faith.

I have considerable respect for those brave souls who maintain the rituals that stop the sky from falling. In particular, they have my respect because, as we all know, Caesar did not, and generally mowed down any and all practitioners of Sky Holding Rituals when he conquered Gaul. We can only suppose that there are still one or two somewhere practicing the rituals, as the sky has not yet fallen. (Thanks be to the Sky Holding Up God- Whoever you are!)

This brings up an important question, is the person with faith sitting on the right better than the one with a different faith sitting beside you on the left at the bar? As a direct example: Can you give an askance look at the primitive stone-worshiping Neanderthal scoffing down his rather poorly made mead and feel superior because YOU believe in the giraffe God of the Mecca Mecca tribe?

In other words, how do we value faith? How do we prove its effectiveness? Here is a small clue: Faith is tested in inverse proportion to its unlikelihood. The more unlikely the thing that you believe in, the greater the faith required to believe it. But here is the paradox: It is a given that the more unlikely a faith the greater is the need to believe in it - Yet in some unknown way this makes it easier to collect adherents. The more absurd and impossible your claim, the more people will clamor to believe in it. This is all part and parcel of the power of faith, some would say gullibility, but nonetheless, it HAS power.

The Power of Faith is a vital thing to consider. Here is the thing, true faith, that pure *'unabiding of any other alternatives blind faith'* in extremely unlikely things, this is like a tremendous magnet to those who WANT to believe. This combination of many people believing in a specific faith both sustains the Gods and gives the people who believe an extraordinary power. To explain: When an entire tribe starts to believe it can walk over hot coals, their faith sustains them, and they can walk over hot coals. But if you happen to have a solitary person wanting to believe it, and they are surrounded by doubters, it is almost impossible for you to do the impossible and walk on hot coals.

So here we find the core difficulty of faith - How do you get the whole thing kicked off? How do you gather enough true believers together in the first place? This is where the Gods come into the picture. Vulcan, for instance, can happily walk over hot coals. In fact, he will chew on them in the morning like they were a crunchy breakfast cereal. If Vulcan requires more faith, faith being essentially the fuel in the tank of the Gods, he might start a fire-walking cult. Here is the thing, you have to PROVE the faith to at least one person. All Vulcan need do is show one important person the power of walking over hot coals, and they then will BELIEVE! Now you have TWO people with faith! All religions are based on a minimum number of two people, and if that if the God and his/her believer, then so be it! That person's faith is infectious and flows out to show other people how it is done - after this the faith quotient goes up until they soon have enough faith that they now can do the impossible.

Here is the point of it all: Vulcan cares not a whit they can walk over coals, it is their FAITH he needs. Faith to the Gods is like food for you and me.

Thus we discover the reason why religions are born. Why religions continue to exist is equally simple, the people need something to have faith in, just as the Gods need someone to believe in them. Just as the Gods need the faith of the people, the people need their faith in the Gods. It is what binds everything together and forms a cohesive society. Without faith, we would all be poking hot coals in the fire, terrified that they will burn us.

This is self-evident when you consider history - as soon as some tribe is overthrown, this tells them that the God they worship is simply not good enough. So they cast him aside, and assume the God of the conquerors. This is common sense because, clearly, this is a better God. After all, it WON. And what happens to the God/s they once believed in? Without anyone having faith enough to support that particular set of Gods, they die! The passage of time is littered with dead Gods.

Such as the God who held up the sky.

Now, I may be wrong, but I suspect the whole 'holding up the sky thing' was a little like tourists at the leaning tower of Pisa - You know how they get in front of the camera and make it look like 'they' are holding it up? It's a trick, an optical illusion, and I would suppose someone like Loki came along and needed a little faith energy for a prank he wanted to do on Thor, so he said to some ignorant Gauls, "Look at me - I am holding up the sky!"

Accordingly, they turn all religious and believe that Loki is the Sky God, and from that point on, they practice their rituals that feed him - it's not such a bad thing when you think about it. No one loses anything, and it gives ignorant Gauls something to do to fill in their days. (Though you can understand why Caesar snorted at their stupidity and killed a good many of them) Which explains why there is no longer a God responsible for holding up the sky, because of the lack of worshippers.

The fact that it stays up is either physics or a miracle. I may be old-fashioned, but I prefer to think of it as a miracle. I know you think me foolish, but let me ask you this: If physics and gravity are the be-all and end-all of everything, why doesn't our atmosphere stratify? Oxygen has a different weight than Nitrogen, and according to all the laws of physics they should stratify into bands of gasses, but they don't!

The explanation given is that the atmosphere is turbulent and keeps mixing everything up, but experiments have been done to test this, isolating our atmosphere in a fish tank affair (They called it something far fancier for the experiment, like an isolation tank) and leaving it for many weeks. Well, even with no turbulence there is still no stratification of gases.

Now, this either proves physics and the principles of gravity wrong, or there is indeed some echo at play of a God who held up the sky. On this point, I am not sure it was his (or her - remember, Celts were even-handed with God Roles) job to stop the atmosphere from stratifying, but then again, maybe it was. Holding up the sky just happened to be a side effect of his/her secretive mixing action.

If this is the case, it may well be that this God has now incarnated as the god of cake mixing and bread kneading. I am not sure of this, but I like to think he (or she) still has a role to play.

The thing is, the BEST faiths are unprovable, unrepeatable, and unbelievable to anyone not of your particular faith. And this is fine because when you truly BELIEVE you KNOW the doubters are wrong. How so? Because they are not of your faith. Catch 22 is now working for you.

For instance, many have faith that Jesus will come again. Apart from this being a little silly (because he never left, and was only recently seen in the vicinity of Valhalla), this is an unprovable faith - therefore holding to it is a distinct feather in the cap of the believer. Conversely, a faith he won't come back is an easy faith, because the evidence is so solidly in its favor. The real question here is, does a LACK of faith improve anything or feed anyone?

Finally, we arrive at the entire purpose of this short essay: It does! Lack of Faith is the NEW RELIGION of the Roman Republic! This anti-faith Faith is the most powerful belief subscribed to by non-believers. People like Trumpetus Rex and Rupus Murdochius are the new high priests of the faithless - the religion based on a reality that serves only one God, a disincarnate entity that is absolutely real, money.

This is a paradox of tremendous proportions, because old faith-based religions, like the Roman religion, are unbelievably rich. They have property assets all over the world that add up to incalculable wealth, and THIS is what Trumpetus Rex wants. He doesn't care about whether you believe, what matters is how much you give him.

His religion is money. His faith is in currency, which is a very easy faith to adhere to. It is a little like the Mithraites believing the Sun is a God, believe or not believe, it still has POWER and we all know that Currency WORKS. You can buy nice things with it, bribe officials to get whatever you want, and what is more, it is VERY easy to get people to believe in cash, therefore adherents are everywhere. It is substantial, you can hold gold. It is universal, everyone will exchange it for whatever you want. It is attractive, science has proven that the smell of money covers up the ugly face and the fat belly and the opposite sex find you amazingly desirable.

The great power of money is that, with enough of it, your will reigns supreme. If you are disgustingly rich not one person will find you disgusting. It is a truly amazing, omnipotent force that can move mountains, because with money you can buy dynamite.

The priests of the Currency God are everywhere, the officials running Lotto Draws, the Mechanics servicing the Poker Machines, the old girl selling raffle tickets at the local school fair - there are all part and parcel of the Money Religion, which believes you CAN get something for nothing and that the truest of Gods is the God of the ATM.

"Ask and you shall receive" is the Money God motto. When you believe in Money, your faith is easily proven because it gets you what you want.

You can easily see the motivation of the new brand of faithless priests like Trumpetus Rex- When he says, "Shove aside the old ways," what he means is that, as the old religions fail, he picks up the property assets. And here I will reveal the greatest power of the faithless religion, the printing press! You don't have to conquer anyone to kill their Gods anymore, you just have to make them look ridiculous. Everything Murdochius published was a way of attacking the old ways through ridicule and innuendo.

Breaking down thousands of years of tradition is no easy thing. In the end, most faith-based beliefs are a little bit like wearing Mickey Mouse ears to protect you from elephants. You know for a fact that elephants are scared of mice, so wearing the mouse ears will keep the elephants out of your room. The subsequent fact that there are no elephants in your room is therefore proof that the mouse ears work.

However, here we come to the truly remarkable thing called "The Leap of Faith". If perchance an elephant DOES enter the room while you are wearing your Mickey Mouse ears, you are entirely within your rights to determine that said elephant is the latest member of your faith. Because, if he isn't, why is he in the room with all the faithful? Logic is on your side.

Further, if said elephant happens to start trampling the faithful, this only proves their faith was not strong enough. Gods have used this 'leap of faith' logic for countless millennia to maintain and keep their followers, but the power of money has been slowly eroding this. This will possibly explain why Odin decided to partner with Jesus. It is plausible that he feared the sarcasm and vicious wit of the printing presses of the Murdocius and hoped the up-and-coming fervor of the Christians might protect them. Why? Because the Christians were certainly not amiss to burning down places that publish things they don't like. In this way, he sought to invigorate his people and bring them back to a little mayhem. The truth was, his people had faded and would get more excited over the opening of a new IKEA store than a sacrifice to Odin.

Only two things were certain in any of the above. The first was that Thor, disguised as a humble blacksmith assistant, had sent a message to Odin that Vulcan was about to do the unthinkable and release the Dragon of Imagination. And the second was that while the Gods just don't care what happened to the plebs, if they got too much imagination, that was a very different story.

For every God knows: If the plebs have unlimited imagination, the one thing they no longer need are Gods to worship. Why is this so? Read on!

Action Stations

Sensing something was up, the Oracle had organized a private audience for her boys. Away from the crowds, she met with Rufus and Ofal, along with her brother, the dear Hercules, and Orpheus. "How was Corinth?" she asked politely, but not really wanting to know, because she already knew. That was a problem with being in the chair of the Pythoness, you pretty much knew the answer to everything, even before you were asked it.

"Corinth was great," replied Rufus, happy to see her but not so happy to have left. "However, Orpheus here was in a terrible hurry to get back here so all I remember now are the bumps."

Ofal chimed in, "Everything would have gone smoothly except for all the bumps. That is the problem with Greek roads, bumps and lumps. Now ROMAN roads, they are ..."

Hercules pushed him aside and gave Meridius a big hug, "Hey baby sister," he bellowed. "Great to see you again!"

"Mmmm," replied Meridius, looking at Orpheus.

Orpheus just coughed, indicating he must speak therefore implying the others should not. When they got the message, he began, "It seems that Vulcan has the Omphalos and will be using it to make magical weapons. I fear he has ill intent towards these God games and is up to something that will unsettle the balance."

Meridius sat and listened intently, as she does, to Orpheus describing the problem with the Omphalos. She sat quietly on her tripod, absorbing the sulfur, considering the options, and waiting for Apollo to speak. Which might take some time, because Apollo was currently panicking and had rushed over to New Rome, right to the cellar of Garam Marsala where Zeus had been downing the last of his very fine wine collection.

But he wasn't there, so he panicked more, and followed the trail of his chariot to a mountain top where he found Zeus walking around stark naked with the most stunning creature he had ever seen, and who looked at him like he was dirt.

Now, in most people's imagination they tend to picture Apollo as a sun bronzed athlete with a deep, bellowing voice, but that was Zeus in earlier days. Most people looking at the REAL Apollo would realize he is quite effeminate with his blonde curly locks and lisp. But on the positive, he was the only God to make the pinup poster for both gay men AND lesbians! "Daddy, Daddy deawest - Tho thorry to interwupt but

Vulcan has the Ompwalos so I sent Mercuwy to have a quick look at what he might be up to - and he has a feather dwagon sitting on it. I fear he means to hatch the Dwagon of Imagination!"

Zeus looks up sardonically, "Well, at least that's one thing no one will ever accuse you of, Apollo, too much imagination." *or too much IQ,* he thought to himself. But then he ran through what this might mean and what it was the Vulcan might be up to. In the dim part of his memory he seemed to recall there was a reason why that Dragon was never hatched, or was it enclosed in magical protections by Merlin? But he was so drunk he could not quite recall.

That is the thing about Gods, they may have mighty powers, but they drink so much the memory is not quite up to par - That is unless you have slighted them, they may have terrible memories, but if they believe you have done something wrong, by the GODS they will never forget it. Just ask Sisyphus.

Before you judge, this is not necessarily a bad thing - after you have lived for thousands of years, if you remember everything the brain gets so crammed full of stuff that you cannot learn new things. And honestly, other than your language, your name, your relatives, (so you can keep track of who wants to stab you in the back), and your role in the scheme of things, what else is there that is SO important that you must remember?

Imagine the brain is a filing system and every memory is a picture that has to be filed into it. The brain's librarian must categorize and classify every single image it receives. Experience teaches us that the vast amount of images we receive have little to no value and we would be a fool to keep them. Ergo, the Gods do not. All this New Age waffle about living in the present? This comes from the Gods, because it is pretty much all they CAN do.

Here is the secret, the thing they hold close and always remember is a grudge, because it not only makes life more interesting, it is a survival clause to ensure you recall those who have done you wrong. Mind you, poor Sisyphus apparently did a terrible wrong to Zeus by cheating death on a couple of occasions, which is the perfect example of the downside to the goldfish memory. Because he only remembers wrongs done to him, Zeus assumes that if he remembered you, you have done him wrong. The truth was, Sisyphus did something remarkable, he cheated death which was why he stayed in the great God's thought.

Yet BECAUSE of this striking feat of excellence, the poor fellow was sentenced to an eternity of rolling a rock up a hill. Why? You see, what the Gods possess is not a memory, but a forgetory. This might seem like a reverse sort of logic, but as a God casts anything into their forgetory, if they remember you then they KNOW you have done them wrong. The logic is simple: Because Zeus forgot he recalled the fellow for doing something astonishing, he automatically put him into the place where enemies go. Therefore Zeus was deaf to any entreaty to the contrary regarding the cruel, inhumane punishment he gave the poor fellow. Why? Because, while it may have been hard to place exactly what the wrong might be, he remembered something, so it must be a grievous wrong.

Now, Zeus retained a vague memory of something to do with an egg and the Dragon of Imagination, so he automatically presumed it was because it had in some way done him wrong, but as it was not a sharp sense of forgotten memory it may not have been such a big deal. However, logic tells you that if you CAN remember something from countless eons ago, then it probably was a bad thing that should be paid attention to - and if he had housed a Dragon inside a rock it was most likely to do with the dragon being the issue.

As he thought of it, he wondered who he might send to have a look and report back. That was when he remembered his relatives (a thing Gods always remember) and that Hades got on very well with Vulcan, so maybe he should send his brother? Ah, but he REMEMBERED this, so maybe the two of them were in a plot against him? That made perfect sense, so logically he should go and get Hades checked out as well? "Vulcan and Hades, hey?" he muttered.

And HERE we see a perfect illustration of how bureaucracy works. The bumbling inadequacy of it all somehow manages to struggle to the exact point of concern BECAUSE of the incompetence, not despite it. Zeus had accidentally fallen into the precise and correct suspicion of what Gods were posing an immediate threat.

At this point, you may be saying to yourself, *"These Gods are a bit like chickens in a coop, just pecking along, with no memory of the past and no concern over the future."* You are entirely correct in this, but with one great difference, Gods are extremely vindictive. It is their bitterness and hatred that motivates them to go past the safe confines of the present moment, and the paradox of it all is that they have these emotions BECAUSE they can't remember anything. The bitter emotions are what maintain the recollection of all that has been done wrong to them - otherwise, they would drink the ambrosia and forget everything.

By this time, Zeus had already forgotten what Apollo had said, and only remembered his suspicion. "Where were we?" he asks Loki, who still looks like Helen.

"You were going to give some order to check out Vulcan and Hades," Loki suggested, finally seeing what might be happening in the background.

He asked, "Who have we got to check out Vulcan and Hades?"

Apollo is ecstatic that daddy has noticed what he spoke about and had decided to act. He is almost beside himself with joy. "I will go myselth!" he announces, full of pride and determination.

Zeus is immediately worried, and though he cannot remember about what, a thought occurs to him, "Can you go see Meridius and see what she reckons?" There, that is the safe course of action. His favorite Oracle can be trusted to sort this out, whatever it might be that this was because he had already forgotten.

It was at this precise point that Meridius sat up on her Tripod and announced, "We will be receiving the God Apollo!"

oooOOOOooo

Gods tend to arrive in a blaze of glory, or so the myths tell us. Indeed they CAN, but while their chariots (should they choose to fly them) blaze away in the sky as bright as a sun, when it comes to visiting temples they don't bother. It is a little like Star Trek where they beam down and materialize, but they appear only if the temple is in good order and offerings of wine and cheese are placed upon the altar to attract them.

Honestly though, the wine and cheese mostly humor the mice. (mice love getting drunk) Gods like Apollo prefer coffee and baklava - and not that rubbish made with sugar, or glucose, but with proper honey. So Meridius sent a runner to fetch these from a local coffee shop while the group made their way up the stairs from the prediction chamber to the house of Apollo above it.

It was a sturdy temple, fairly bare and austere, apart from all the woven gold tapestries, the fresh flowers, and the gold offerings that littered the place. In normal cities, this would have had a hundred thieves a day trying their luck, but in Delphi, there was SO much gold everywhere, you tended to forget it was worth stealing.

Plus it was a bank - no one questioned you taking gold IN, but everyone stared at you when you took it OUT. Truth to tell, no one ever took gold out from Delphi, they didn't need to. In this, the place was remarkable - You could fund an entire war with the agreement to move gold from one point in Delphi to another point. This mysterious mechanism was one where you could say to an Athenian shipbuilder, "I want twenty fighting ships!" and simply tell your priest in Delphi to move a specific amount of gold from your votary altar in the Temple of Athena to HIS votary altar in the Temple of whoever.

When this chit was signed at the Temple of Whoever, a raven was sent, and you suddenly had all the money you needed to build twenty warships. This might seem normal to any who deals with international trade, but in Delphi, there was a major difference - If the Oracle wanted to stop a war, she might not authorize the release of that Chit and call for the arguing parties to see her. One of the things so many people said about Meridius was how extraordinarily good she was at stopping wars and finding negotiated settlements.

However, none of this applied when it came to arguments between the Gods - which is when you think about it, ironic. The entire world operated on diplomacy via the various Temples in Delphi, yet the Gods these Temples were devoted to paid no heed to them. No, they paid heed to things like fine wine and good times, and in the case of Apollo, coffee and sweets.

As the aroma of the freshly brewed beverage wafted through the shrine the golden hair of Apollo started to come out of the mist that had formed behind the altar. "And BAKLAVA!" he exclaimed with delight, reaching from the same cloud to bring the syrupy indulgence to his lips. "Mmmm, ahh, oohhh that is good." Then a sip of the coffee, "Ahhh, it is SO nice to be back in the human realm. Thank you darlings. Up on Mount Olympus, it is all ambrosia, ambrosia, ambrosia - you get so tired of it. Not a decent coffee to be found, I have no idea why people think it is such a great place."

Then the God Apollo appeared to grasp that there were others in the shrine, "Oh, you have people with you Meridius?"

"Yes, Appy - You know my brother, The Ogoglio. (he nods) I believe you have met Orpheus? (he nods again, indicating to get on with it) Hercules, of course, though we call him Brutus Maximus at the moment. (Apollo gives a grimace of a smile, he definitely knows Hercules) The others are friends here to help out. So what do we have on the Omphalos?"

"Darling, Zeus sends his regards, and says he wants you to sort everything out."

Meridius just looked at him, going, "mmmm?" with a question inside it.

"Ok, he wants me to sort it, but he said to see what you think about it all. But we all know, you are the only capable one around here, so please sort it out." Now, two things. The first is you will be asking where his gay lisp has gone? Well, that is because he is so nervous around his father, here on Earth he was far more confident. Second, you might imagine a God like Apollo might be a bit miffed being questioned by a human like Meridius, but not at all. Most of the Gods considered her to be the mother they always wished they had, and her knowing looks and wise ways were a comfort to them, in particular to Apollo, who had a nervous temperament.

"So," he continued, "the story is that Zeus thinks Hades has done a deal with Vulcan, and Mercury tells me that Vulcan is going to hatch the Omphalos and release the Dragon of Imagination. Oh, and Merlin has been caught in a magic canceling net, so he can't help."

The Oracle thought long and hard, then asked, "Have you any idea what the Dragon of Imagination will do once he is hatched?"

Apollo was surprised, "I would suppose he spreads imagination all over the place?"

Meridius chimed in, "And Appy darling, what will THAT do?"

"I have no idea, but from your tone, I gather it is not good." Apollo was not yet fully engaged in the conversation because the baklava was still being finished.

"All the Gods will die, chaos will emerge, and darkness shall consume the world - you know, all the things you folk fought against at the beginning of time? The only thing left will be Hades." Meridius explained.

Apollo wrinkled his perfect nose, "That would be awful. The underworld is horrid and dull."

Vampires

A generally unseen group of individuals that live between the elevated status of Godhood and the common status of man are the vampires. Contrary to popular opinion, they do not suck blood, and any such notion should be immediately cast aside. They do not even live in the physical realm but in a place commonly known as the Astral Regions, or the planes of emotions.

You see, what vampires like to eat are EMOTIONS. They come closest to the human realm in dreams, and they suck off the terror of nightmares, the lust of sex dreams, or the hope found in some happy dream. Raw emotion is what sustains them, but they prefer it flavored with fear or dread, or best of all, the emotions of love. Everyone loves to suck off those who fall in love, which explains why it never lasts - for the poor lovers are getting their love pulled out of them and sucked up by any one of a dozen vampires living in their community.

The other thing vampires particularly like is the emotion of sport. The emotion of sport? What could these be? (you may well ask) If you ask this question, you have not been to an English football match. For some unknown reason, humans get extremely excited to see other people doing things, such as kicking a ball from one end of the field to another. It is this excitement that pulls the vampires in, and for those with the eyes to see, they appear as shadowy figures behind emotionally stirred people. As they suck up the energy they are fed in much the same way as Gods are when you offer them prayers and your faith.

Yes, they are living vicariously off others, but is it such a bad thing? Few could argue against the fact that humans have far too many emotions, and the existence of vampires ensures a balance of sorts. Plus, as they are always so close to individuals, they gather a tremendous amount of information. In particular, one of the vampires living off the Trumpetus Rex had come back to the chief administrator of vampire business with a very disturbing tale about dragons being hatched.

After close listening, that particular administrator immediately rushed upstairs to the head of emotion collecting, bypassing the superintendents of Fear, Guilt, and Shame, and going straight to the man in charge of Religion. That office had, needless to say, been heavily invested in procuring emotional discharges since time immemorial. Anthropologists who seek to find the instigating cause for religion always overlook this simple, salient fact: It was the vampires organizing it all.

The Vampires were the ones who first went to the ugly little crew of immortals living on top of their mountain, and suggested everything could be made better with a bit more faith energy pouring into the coffers. What God could refuse more faith? It was agreed that the vampires could serve this purpose and if you think for a moment, "Who would do a deal with a vampire?" - Well, being Gods, they didn't think much at the best of times, and with the sweet nectar of more faith being handed out, they didn't need to think at all.

Which is why the Vampires created religion.

Religion became the single greatest force that not only fed the Gods, but the vampires as well. They also helped to organize and form religious institutions into the heavily bureaucratic organizations they are today. To explain: For a vampire administrator, religion is looked on as units of energy. A small little cult on the fringe of some community might have maybe twenty adherents, given that the average faith energy is one human power per person, then this is twenty units of faith power going up to the God who is worshipped. This is quite simple, and yes, some super fervent believer might kick in an extra unit or two, but there will be some laggard merely there for the sex, so it all balances out.

It is the LAGGARD the vampires focused on. They loved all that forbidden energy given off by the people who went around betraying the principles of their religion and committing adultery. And here is the real brilliance of the vampire plan - To make sex outside of marriage something terrible, and inside marriage something impossible.

I get a tad excited when I think of the utter cleverness of what they did, they merged chaos into order and fooled absolutely everyone in the process. They told the Gods that to get more faith energy, a little procreation was needed. All very innocent, the Gods say, "Sure, that makes sense."

The next step, convince the Gods that society will be better organized if people are MARRIED, and best to make THAT part of the religion as well. The Gods can see nothing wrong with this notion so they tick it off as approved.

After this comes the final nail in the coffin of happiness, the vampires argue that as the Gods are all about order over chaos, which cannot be argued against, they say, "Therefore we need to make certain that the humans behave, thus we make a rule that once you are married you can only have sex with your partner."

This caused a little consternation, to which the vampire hastily added, "Not that this applies to GODS, of course. They are ABOVE those sorts of shenanigans."

The foolish Gods agreed, not seeing the clever plan behind it all. Once this third stage of the plan was introduced, the vampires started whispering into the ears of the people that would become the rulers of these new churches, "Your job is to maintain order and ensure a constant supply of faith to the Gods."

Well, who could say this was incorrect? It was indeed the governing principle of the priestcraft that the vampires created. Find the most sanctimonious and arrogant members of society, place them in a position over everyone else, and call them priests. It was perfect, no royal blood needed, just sufficient ignorance welded to arrogance, after which you can take a common man and set them on a pulpit where they can start to tell everyone what is right or wrong.

Are you beginning to appreciate the deep and enormous wisdom the vampires had in their souls? (or lack of soul, as the case may be) Step by step they set up a structure that would provide them food for eternity, or as long as any particular religion lasted. Now if you think this is callous, I ask you, is it callous of a farmer to use a horse to plow his field? He has enslaved another creature to do his bidding so that he and his family can eat. But the horse doesn't mind, he quite enjoys his life, out in the sun, breathing country air.

No, callous is the boss employing people to sit in offices, breathing air conditioning, performing mundane and utterly boring tasks, then paying them barely enough to survive. Against all this the vampires were positively generous: They created employment, supplied faith to the gods, and only harvested a little of the fun energy that occurred on the side.

It was the "fun energy" they were after. Yes, you may call it guilty pleasure, hedonism, or perversion, but really, it was just the energy that vampires liked to eat. They are not interested in FAITH, which is bland and boring. Eating faith all day long is like a brown rice diet with no Chinese food to go with it. They wanted something spicy, and the way they got this was a thing of beauty indeed.

After creating religion and creating a priestcraft, they then set about creating RULES for humans. We all know people are unruly until someone put them in order, and so the vampires created a world where people got ordered by rules and ruled by rulers. After you corral sheep into a paddock, you need a sheepdog to maintain order and get them through into the shearing shed, so that all your efforts are made worthwhile.

Sadly, this is all humans represent to gods and vampires - they are a thing to be regularly shorn of excess energy, and to do this, you have to keep them in order. That is IT! Here we have the entire purpose and need for religion. And before you argue how unfair this all seems, find me a sheep that does not WANT to be shorn! They like it, they want it, and they discovered letting everyone else tell them what to do was very pleasing as it took any burden of responsibility off their shoulders.

But the REAL secret and why the vampires went to so much trouble was because, in their rules for this new religion, they inserted the clause that made everything worthwhile. This rule was, "Thou shalt not commit adultery!"

Beautiful! Everyone knows you get bored with your partner after a couple of years. First, it is all hot and raunchy, but then it gets repetitive and you start to look for better sex elsewhere. That sister of the wife, she is pretty, maybe she is interested? But it is FORBIDDEN, and while you skulk around the edges, feeling guilty about what you have done or are thinking of doing, yet loving it, there you find the vampires, harvesting all your guilt and longing.

This is the true harvest for the vampires. Hidden, guilty pleasure is a feast for them. It provides a HUGE bank of energy that can feed whole colonies of vampires, and not just for vampires of lust. Everyone enjoys guilt and shame, it is the salt and pepper of the vampire diet.

At this point, we should note that the vampire community was in overdrive with the coming games. You see, the vampire bank can also take in emotions from the Gods themselves. One lightning blast of Zeus contained enough anger to support a tribe of vampires for months, and so they were all eagerly looking forward to the destruction, I mean, games.

Because of this, the Vampire in charge of Religion, that money-sucking creature called Dracula, did not at first get the urgency. In fact, he didn't see a problem at all: "So what if Vulcan is hatching a Dragon of Imagination? More imagination means more fears, it can only be good for the feeding of our brothers.

The chief administrator of vampire business just shook his head. Dracula, whose nickname was Spatula, because he was always scraping things from the bottom of the barrel, had been sucking on the fumes of religion too long. These are potent energies and dangerous to the intellect - The scent of "I am right and you are wrong" that all religions carry eventually affects your thinking, dulling the mind so all imagination leaves and only dogma remains.

"It is not about feeding off anything, it is about having something to feed off when it is done! Vulcan's plan is to kill off the Gods. That means religion dies, and we are back sucking off some lonely little swineherd for breakfast. Do you not see WHY the Dragon of Imagination is the thing the Gods fear most?" he suggested, trying to guide the foolish vampire to clear thinking.

"Exactly!" announced Dracula. "They FEAR it, so it will give us even more energy to suck on. This is fantastic news, people will have their imaginations unleashed, they will discover how powerful they are, and at the same time their repressed subconscious selves will be imagining all sorts of blocks to stop them, therefore the harvest of energy will be incredible. I can't see why you would be so depressed."

The chief administrator of vampire business was called Ekatahuna, which curiously is the same name for a tiny little town in the middle of the North Island of New Zealand. Because nothing ever happened there some believed the town was named after him. In this case, Ekatahuna came prepared, knowing what a fool Dracula was. He pulled out charts of projected emotional harvest expectations, and at first pointed to the bit where they are all going up - higher than they had ever been. "This is what you are looking at?"

"See! What did I tell you?" Dracula laughed.

Then Ekatahuna turned the page, which showed a precipitous drop in the emotional harvest - down to net ZERO inside two years. "But I don't understand - it was going so well. How could it drop to nothing?"

Ekatahuna sighed, "Because everyone dies. That is the result of Vulcan releasing the Dragon of Imagination, as uncontrolled imagination leads to one result, the annihilation of all life on the planet. THIS is why the Gods housed it in the first place - it is the tool of chaos."

"But, but - imagination is what FEEDS us! Every schoolboy vampire is taught that the seeds of emotion come from the imagination of the humans, and we TICKLE their imagination, to get them to emote! By the Gods, we are the muses of the whole world, tickling the creatives to write a song that sways an entire populace, then we live off all that energy they create. It has been a perfect circle, how could imagination kill off the planet?" Dracula is shocked - everything he has ever known has been thrown into a quandary.

"You do not understand. People imagining things means nothing, normally. Stirs the emotions, we collect a tithe, imagining comes to nothing or maybe a nice little song. But when empowered by the Dragon of Imagination, whatever you imagine will happen.

"A LITTLE imagination is good. Thank the Gods that the populace is so stupid and so lacking in imagination. We muse a few creatives to stir the emotions, but what happens if that the dragon turns EVERYONE into a creative genius? Competition is what happens. As soon as Bob at 24 grasps they can imagine a red Ferrari in their drive and BOOOM, it is there - So what does Stan at 26 do? He imagines a Pink Porsche, maybe THREE pink Porsches. And number 28 imagines ten Lamborghinis.

Then number 30 hates the noise of high performance sports cars revving so loudly, so HE imagines he has a Mack truck that runs over all of them." Ekatahuna explained.

"Now imagine what happens when every street in every town in every country starts doing the same? The entire world starts getting overcrowded with the things people imagined they wanted, like gym equipment, but never used - so they throw it out. This causes an ungodly clogging of all the pathways and byways on the planet, and soon enough there are no streets left to even drive a Mack truck over things to squash them.

"And after that? People start to go crazy and imagine large guns and atomic weapons, trying to do something to stop neighbors crowding out their life with all that junk. Then they start to hurt each other, screaming at the neighbor to stop imagining crap. Everyone knows they have to stop, but they can't. They are addicted to imagining the next best thing! Now all the intruding garbage that is pushed into people's faces sets the world on the path of imagining revenge. People start thinking of bigger and better ways to kill each other, and the recrimination grows until the entire world becomes a killing field. The vendettas and feuds run until there is but one person left, the last remnant of imagination, and the WINNER of the contest! But soon that last person expires from loneliness and regret."

"But surely the Gods will intervene? I mean, that is their job!" Dracula protested.

"Well no. That is the point, the flip side of humans having unlimited imaginations is that they dream of something and it manifests - DER! They no longer need to pray to some hidden God, and they certainly don't need to go to church, because now THEY are Gods. The result of unlimited imagination for all is that the Gods will expire because all faith energy will cease, so they starve and drop like lemmings over a cliff. The result of my statistics are clear: Release the Dragon of Imagination, and the world ends in under two years."

And here was the real point of all this, a thing that needed to be explained carefully because Dracula was an idiot, "And so, what happens to us? Like the Gods, we all starve. Yes, we start out with an almighty feast, but soon existence will fade and our shades will go to the underworld. There we will ALL be, arguing with each other in the eternal shadows."

Dracula is distraught, "By the Gods, not the underworld? It is SO BORING! But if all the Gods die, how come Hades will still exist?"

"Because that particular God has absolutely no imagination at all. It's all flails and whipping and pushing rocks up hills in utter pointlessness. Plus he doesn't need faith energy, he doesn't need anything but death. He loves watching people starve and suffer, that is what feeds him!"

Dracula protested, "But why is Vulcan doing this? Surely he can see what will happen?"

Ekatahuna just blinked his eyes, "Have you ever met Vulcan?"

Dracula received enlightenment, "Oh yes. A miserable son of a bitch. His emotions taste terrible - Hates everyone, never smiles, grumpy all the time."

"Not exactly true, he smiled when he announced his plan to Hades."

"Oh dear," said Dracula, understanding at last just how serious a problem they had. "What can we do about it?"

oooO000ooo

What to do indeed? Because of his brilliance in grasping the seriousness of the problem, Ekatahuna had been given the problem to solve. He, of course, was a bureaucrat whose singular claim to fame was an extraordinary lack of imagination. Plus he was remarkably incompetent, so this whole putting him in charge of saving everything was perhaps not a wise course of action. But graphs do not lie, unless you put them upside down, and right now Ekatahuna was wishing his graphs were upside down.

Here he had a singular thought, the one notion that might save the entire world: The vampire Ekatahuna recognized his total and complete inadequacy. This might seem to oppose the notion of saving the world, however, understanding he could not deal with the situation meant that he then wondered who or what might, which left room for the concept that Meridius was the Oracle, therefore it was her job to find insights to solve things!

How he came to this extraordinary leap of awareness, who can say? Perhaps it is proof of God? (Other than you could go to Mount Olympus and meet a bevy of them) Perhaps it was centuries of experience with the Oracle solving things, but Ekatahuna knew in his (lack of) bones this was the answer.

But how to get this information to the Oracle? The problem here was she had only extremely positive emotions - nothing a vampire could feed off or connect to. Her goodness polarized the air around her and would make it almost impossible for Ekatahuna to get close enough to whisper suggestions into her ear. This is how vampires work, they whisper thoughts to you, give you clues, and try to lead you in a direction that feeds them.

But if they don't like the taste of your emotions, forget it. This brings up an entirely unrelated point, the uselessness of books on positive mental thinking. Despite what all the motivational books say about positive thinking, no vampire worth his salt will help a person soaked in totally positive vibes. Pure Positive emotions simply taste awful to a vampire. Being positive is nice in theory, but very bad in practice.

This explains why rude, crude, and truly abrasive people are so often rich, because vampires love to feast on their negative emotions, and will whisper to their clients ways to go in order to generate money, knowing this is the source of the all negative emotion.

Perhaps I need to explain? Vampires feed off your emotions, and we have covered this, but to get better emotions to feed off, they will assist miserable and horrid people into positions of authority and power. Do-gooders and saints have no flavor at all - their kindness and unconditional love make their emotions bland. Plus they tend to have angels around them, and as everyone knows, angels and vampires do not get on.

Ekatahuna held a tremendous suspicion that the angels around the saints and good people were sucking up their goodness just as his kind sucked up the vile and despicable feelings, but it was hard to prove, and why would you bother? Who cared if angels liked the syrupy sweetness of persons like Meridius and Orpheus?

They far preferred the more complex flavors of A: someone pretending to be good, while at heart they were horrid, or B: the foolish flavors of those who were very bad, but who thought they were good - these were the type of intense emotions that true vampires preferred. If a vampire found a child with this sort of potential, they went out of their way to arrange things in the external world that would encourage the growth of this complexity. In this, the best vampires were very much like winemakers, cultivating, pruning, and over time harvesting the crop of emotional outpouring from an individual.

Which explains the extraordinary rise of the Trumpetus Rex and Rupus Murdochius. They were the perfect combination of "A" and "B". As such, the pair had an entire bevy of vampires surrounding them. Not to mention the ones that hooked onto the groveling supplicants of the pair.

I must pause and answer the question I feel is in the air. If vampires do not feed of positive emotions, why do they hang around people who are in love? Well, this simply underlines your lack of understanding of what "In Love" truly is. There is not one single case in the entire world of two people staying "In Love" for any great length of time. This is because being "In Love" is an outright and outrageous lie: You are blinded to the persons shortcomings and faults, and you see everything they do as glorious.

As the Vampires suck the illusion from your thoughts, you start to see reality. The beer swilling pig you thought was Adonis is in fact, a beer swilling pig. This is not to say you cannot accommodate this because, to be fair, what HE saw was a wondrous angel, not the nagging hag you are. As you learn to lower your expectations you might even develop a vague sense of affection for the person, and therefore form a lasting bond. But remember, bond and bondage, not a whole lot of difference.

On the technical side of things, Vampires come in five main types, defined by the passion they most prefer. This five are listed as Lust, Anger, Vanity, Greed, and best of all, Attachment - with all the procrastination and avoidance of responsibility this involved. Ekatahuna was an attachment vampire, therefore people who were industrious and busy achieving things were energetically opposed to him - which was another reason why he felt he would not be able to get close to Meridius.

But it seems he would have to try - the fate of the world depended on it.

Now at this point, we must remember that all the statistics and analyses of the vampires were just projections, but as you can always count on the power of human depravity, they had never been wrong. Even so, they do not account for the GOOD people, as they have absolutely no connection to them. It was entirely possible that releasing the Dragon of Imagination would be very good for the good, and very bad for the bad. This would mean all evil would depart this world and it would become an earthly paradise.

However, if we count up all the truly good people in the world, that would mean perhaps a few dozen will survive - this would not be very good for the bad and, when you think about it, not so good for the good because who will run the Italian restaurants? Plus if you DID get into a legal argument, there would be no solicitors left.

Based on this logic, I feel we can all presume that something had to be done.

But what?

Hercules

We have all heard the soothsayers proclaiming, "The Fates have decreed!" People love to use this term as if they understand what it might mean. The truth is, very few understand the Fates, nor their purpose, nor their decrees. Further, not one person puts forward a decent explanation as to why a few women with spinning wheels have so much influence over human existence.

You will be surprised to learn that the Fates came into existence because there were no cats on Mount Olympus. What do you get when three lonely women need company, but there is no cat for them to pamper? The Fates: vindictive, callous Fates that is what you get. Three screaming banshees full to the brim of bitterness and spite.

This also explains why Mad Cat Ladies continue to exist, because they are the favorites of the Fates. No one in their right mind wants a mad cat woman living next door - Humans developed the entire concept of town councils specifically to be able to set up rules to moderate crazy cat ladies. You know the ones, you walk past the yard that stinks of cat piss, saying "Good afternoon," to the mad woman as a courtesy, and she echoes back at you, "Afternoon, afternooooon!"

She might then explain how she is going into town to talk to the local supermarket owner about borrowing three million dollars, and you are left to wondering why, so you foolishly ask, "You are buying a new house?"

To which she responds, "Afternooon, afternoooon!"

Crazy Cat Women take out large loans because cats are so expensive to feed. The thing about crazy cat women is that invariably their roof leaks, their kitchen needs replacement, and their fences need mending. But suggest to them that they stop feeding the cats and repair their house and they look at you as if YOU are insane.

Which is when you start to ask why the Fates have allowed it. The answer may surprise: They WANT crazy cat women disturbing the fabric of time and space because their particular brand of madness is what opens the world to their influence. Every crazy cat woman you meet is a portal for the evil nature of the Fates.

It is harder to explain why the Fates hated Heracles so much, however.

Brutus Maximus, or Hercules as the Romans knew him, was a very unlikely hero. Apart from the accident of being born a Demi-God, Brutus had only one goal he sought to achieve, which was drinking and partying. Two goals, you suggest? To Hercules, drinking and parties were the same thing. Some might think this a facile waste of a life, with all the depth and integrity of a tonight show host, but underneath this bland front deep currents flowed.

(Disclaimer: All the tonight show hosts who are wise enough to invite this narrator on to talk about this book are naturally excluded from this ridicule.)

The thing about Hercules that few fail to grasp is how he understood the Fates and could negotiate their ways. His simple understanding that he had no control over anything at all meant he didn't resist them. His utter helplessness before their power combined with his incredible strength is what saved him from innumerable situations where his line of fate would have normally been snipped.

There is an ancient question some have asked: Was Hercules a Demi-God because Zeus mated with a human, or was there some other criteria? I feel there is an obvious thing many have overlooked - What makes a man into a God is his ability to resist the string of his fate being snipped. If you do not die, surely this has to be a significant contributor to your God Quotient?

The Fates, Gods bless 'em, are nasty pieces of work that delight in killing people. Consider, you have your line of fate, things are going swimmingly, then SNIP - dead. They pull out the scissors and cut you off from the wellspring of life. However, if your string is too tough, or you are too wily, or if any number of things occur that stop your string from getting snipped, you will stay alive. Do this for long enough, and there you are, a GOD.

And yet, the paradox - Gods can die, and often have. What I suspect is that the Zeus gene gave the baby Hercules super human resilience. This means that when the Fates went to snip his string, it is too tough to cut. The other consideration is that when you are as strong as Brutus Maximus, it is seriously difficult for you to die, as you have a sort of bear reflex that strikes out and thumps anything in your vicinity when you are challenged.

Bears are not very good at clever conversation, nor do they have refined table manners, snatching at the salmon plate as they do. They are also apparently quite stupid and almost totally unable to do a crossword. Plus they love to sleep. All these things describe Brutus Maximus so perfectly, you would be forgiven for thinking he was a bear. Have you ever argued with a bear? If you are still here, likely, you haven't.

Now perhaps it is time to reveal the terrible and sad story of Hercules. It is little known, crowded out with the more spectacular myths that are talking about the seven labors of Hercules - We all know the stories, how he beat up a lion, that sort of thing. This is mostly media PR because the REAL story is quite tragic.

You see, when Zeus first met baby Hercules, he remembered something - This memory came from the fact the baby was a relative, but he didn't look like one. Being as Gods only remember when someone has done them wrong, Zeus presumed Hercules was an enemy. Having NO NOTION what-so-ever that it was his son, he instructed the Fates to deal with the little creature, which is another way of saying, "Kill the baby."

But Hercules had this inordinately strong Fate Line. When they went to snip it, even their sharpest scissors could not manage it. So what they did was haul on the string, and drag Hercules into their domain. What they did not count on was how strong he was, and instead of dragging him into their world, he dragged them into ours. But there was collateral damage - everyone and everything connected the Heracles (to the Greeks he was Heracles) got caught up in his fate line, and got pulled into the realm of Fate.

He meets a new girl, they start to fall in love, and BAM, she is dragged off by the Fates, and Hercules is left standing there alone. This was the true tragedy - Everyone he knew got dragged off, and as you crossed the line from this world into the land of fate, your line of fate is snipped. Imagine it, everyone you love and care for is hauled off, and every day you wake alone.

No reason is given, and worse, you wake up with no memory of the event, just the vague sense that something is missing - for when the fates snip your line, it is like you never existed. It is WHY people build statues, to set in stone their memory so that no matter what the fates might do, they will be remembered. The Lord Mayor of some little town improves its sewage, so he convinces the town clerk that he should be honored for his great achievement with a statue. In the minds of many, this is the only form of immortality open to man.

A woman will have children, for THEY will remember her when she is gone, no matter what the fates might do. A young man dreams of writing the great play, for in this way HE shall be remembered. Everyone wants to 'make their mark' not for money but for MEMORY.

Is it not then a tremendous paradox and irony that the Gods have almost no memory? Perhaps this is a necessary part of achieving godhood, forgetting the past completely? It is a curious thought that has been puzzled here, and I admit, I cannot find an answer to it. Obviously,

I would stop and ask a God about this, but herein lies yet another paradox, they wouldn't remember! Worse, if they did they would look at you suspiciously and give you a rock to roll up a hill.

In the case of Hercules, he made a terrible mistake. Many hundreds of years ago a terrible fate, the worst of all possibilities, was handed out to him - the fate of undying love.

The Fates are jealous creatures - When they saw that the one they could never defeat (Hercules) found deep and abiding happiness in the arms of a woman, they went crazy. You must understand, Hercules was the one mortal who was stronger than they were. No matter how much they tried to drag him into their realm, he would instinctively fight back, and the next thing they would come tumbling head over heels into the human world.

His great strength and enormous heart overcame even Fate, or so it might seem.

But when his one, great, undying love vanished, leaving no trace of her memory (for her fate line was snipped) a great hole was left behind. Wherever Hercules went, he kept going back to see what he had lost. He had no idea what it was, but he knew he had lost something! This left the Demi-god in a state of confusion. He KNEW there was something important he needed to remember, but for the life of him, he couldn't.

As the fates rolled out their plan pulling him into Fate World, killing off everything Hercules loved, then getting themselves dragged out into this world, the ongoing struggle wore down his memory until it finally caused poor Hercules to forget everything. He woke up in a field of war and all the soldiers presumed he was one of theirs who must have had a hit on the head. When Hercules came to he believed he was a Roman soldier called Brutus Maximus.

But what happened to the Fates, you ask? They had to get back to their world and to do this, the Fates would have to grant some human a boon, which is where the three wishes from the genie business came about. You have all heard the story, the Genie appears, grants you three wishes, and the first wish is invariably, "What should I wish for?"

BOOM, one down, two to go.

The smarter humans wish for unlimited wishes, but that sort of hubris just annoys the Fates and they hold up their scissors suggesting that the first wish should be one where they don't die, because unlimited wishes only last as long as the life of the petitioner. Honestly, if you can't cram everything you want and need into a single wish, you are not very bright. So, should a Genie appear and grant you three wishes, I suggest the following:

"I wish for a beautiful male/female human partner (don't forget to name both the sex and species or you might end up with a cat) who adores me and wants to be with only me, but who will bend the rules occasionally with threesomes, who has millions and millions of ounces of Gold they are happy to share throughout both of our very long lives as we live in a wonderful country totally lacking in inflationary influences where you don't get called up to serve in the armed forces."

As a first wish, this pretty much ticks most of the boxes, and if the fates want to nitpick and say this is many wishes rolled into one, you can say, "Then you just agreed this was one wish!" and if they hold up their scissors you qualify it, saying, "Ok, I want a beautiful HUMAN soul with me, I want money, and I want a nice place to live!"

In this way, you don't look too much like a smart arse and there is a possibility they may even give you these things and not a stunted dwarf donkey with gold teeth that lives in a lovely stable. But I warn you, if you challenge them, you will lose, unless you are Hercules. When they saw he was deeply in love, the three women became openly enraged, because over the years of fighting him, after repeatedly trying to snip his fate line, they had come to fancy him. And the thought of losing him to another woman sent them a little mad.

They went, "Noooo!" and pulled on the string of his Fate so hard that anyone who had any connection to him was drawn into the maelstrom - one that only he could survive where no ordinary human could. As he walked away from the storm, he did the most remarkable thing - for he saw his Line of Fate, the thing that was drawing him into all the terrible experiences, and he snipped it with his sword, thinking it was an ordinary rope tying him to what was a bit of a mess.

I mean, who wouldn't? If you had a rope tied to you that appeared to be dragging you underwater, of course you would snip it. Here is the thing, the secret no one will ever tell you, and I have to whisper it and just hope that the Fates do not hear. Cup your hands to your ears, for this whisper is only for you.

"The person who snips their own fate becomes immortal"

But there is a cost, the cost every God pays, a lack of memory. Hercules at that moment forgot everything, he forgot his name, he forgot he was the son of Zeus, he forgot who he was, where he was, and any reason he had to exist was also gone from his brain. Which turned out to be one of the great tragedies for Hercules at that time was a poet who was almost finished his great epic, the "Song of Hercules" called Without Within.

I will remind you of this famous saga:

Without Within
Without Beyond, there is no Beneath
Without Beneath, there is no Between
Without Resistance, there is no Gratitude
Without Constraint, there is no Strength
Without Fear and Doubt, there are no Champions
Without Suffering, there is no Appreciation
Without Beyond, there is no Beneath
Without Beneath, there is no Between
Without Between, there is no Betwixt
Yet, Betwixt Between there is ...

Scholars had long argued over what the last word (or words) should be. Would it be a negative or a positive? Does the poem resolve in harmony or end in angst? The entire context of the necessity of opposites and the juxtaposition of opposing values as being a benefit, not a fault, had stirred whole new philosophies into being. Of course, nothing to match the "Plate It" school of cuisine, but even so, it was an influential work that had far-reaching consequences.

Whole books had been written about the true meaning of Without Within while the notion of Betwixt Between had entire mystery schools devoting many student hours to the study of what it might be. This may seem a touch arrogant of me, but I say the real pivot point of the work is the "Without Beyond, there is no Beneath" bit. It is the opening line and repeated on line Eight, therefore indicative of the Octave, the repeat note higher up the scale. You are expected to have lifted your consciousness to read above the lines. And what is above the lines? For one, common sense tells us it 'should' be "Without Above, there is no Beneath".

But Hercules was not speaking in three dimensions, above and below are a 3D model - No, he speaks of BEYOND! It is the promise of something in the distance, something outside our present reality, and so WITHOUT Beyond, we have nothing. Obviously, this is an oblique reference to constantly being pulled into the realm of fate and the whole poem is about this abiding struggle for existence.

Without this within us, there is nothing underneath our existence to anchor our hearts. But I digress and fall into the fault of philosophizing when I am supposed to be story telling - for there is a very great difference between the two. The STORY is that the truth of all this poetry business is that there was no philosophy at all and that Hercules was merely in love and prattling on about nothing as lovers will do.

Let me put you out of your misery, how the last line ends is no mystery at all! It is a sappy love poem, and what he meant to write was, "only you." The so-called ode is a poem of no great construction of purpose, a flight of whimsy from a fellow more used to inscribing people and things with a sword rather than paper with a pen. And yet, the poignancy of the moment, with the fates pulling his one true love away at a crucial time, and him snipping his line of Fate, thus becoming Immortal, thus becoming a God, all this makes these last words powerful and full of portent. The fact he didn't write them also meant his memory started to fail.

Perhaps it was the shock, perhaps she was only a passing interest and the tearing apart only made it seem such a great loss, but the effect of the event was to both elevate Hercules to Divinity, and paradoxically remove from his mind all knowledge of this fact. He woke on the battle field, naked, and the men there hastily clad him in Roman Armor, presuming he was a member of the military. Subsequent to this, his self-evident ability to wipe out whole battalions on his own meant he was elevated to a high rank and the title of "Maximus" was bestowed on him.

He couldn't remember his name, so the local centurion jokingly called him Brutus, thus Brutus Maximus found himself happily ensconced in the famous nineteenth battalion, and made quite a career for himself. But he wandered off from his squad to drink beer, then he forgot where they were. He ended up taking a job to protect a fur trader, traveling with him to Canadia, where hundreds of years later he comes across Meridius, who helped him start the slow process of recalling who he was.

Here is the important bit, the next time he meets Zeus it is with Meridius (whom all the Gods love) and so there is no association in the mind of Zeus to Heracles/Hercules/Brutus Maximus being an enemy. Rather, he sees Hercules as one of the relatives - which he was. Which explains why he was not cursed with a thousand new impossible quests.

Are we up to date?

The point of all of the above is to highlight that we are very much affected by our influences. Ever since meeting Meridius, apart from starting to remember who and what he was, Brutus Maximus was being bathed in good intentions. Meridius was a paragon of good will to all, she never thought badly of anyone, and everyone got on with her. Conversely, no one ever got on with Hercules unless they were providing drinks or behind him in a battle, and they were happy for him to get on with it.

But when he met the Oracle, everything in his life changed for the better. This was the *Meridius Effect*, her goodness rubbed off on you. It also gave you protection from vampires, and meeting her snipped a connection Hercules had with a very powerful vampire, one called

Acytosis. This one was sucking on the aura of awe that surrounded the great Hercules. Acytosis was siphoning off the faith energy from the people who worshipped the strength of Hercules, for there were still souls who offered praise and prayer to the great one.

When Hercules met Meridius, this connection between vampire and faithful adherent was broken. He started to remember who he was, thus there was no empty space for the vampire to sneak into. This upset the fellow and he put in a complaint to Vampire Administration, and being a bureaucracy these things take a fairly long time to be processed. And here is the miracle bit, for just as the Vampire Ekatahuna was wondering what to do, that very complaint came across his desk, titled, "Theft of connection to Hercules".

NOW do you see the point of the apparently distracted dialogue about Hercules? Meridius was so good that only goodness surrounded her, and even her friends became good, or at least, a lot better than they had been.

The only person around Meridius at that moment who was not specifically "good" was Brutus Maximus. And it is not that he thought he was BAD, no bad people ever think they are bad, but when you think of how many people he had slaughtered and how he considered killing a sport, it is difficult to imagine he was Good. (Though he was very good at killing)

The thing is, Brutus had not killed anyone lately and was building up a wave of goodness around his heart. The Meridius Effect had snipped the vampire Acytosis from his regular feed, and this was the cause of the complaint, but now that was incidental. Ekatahuna saw an opportunity rearing up its golden behind and sent for this Acytosis, who arrived, shortly thereafter - bad tempered and looking hungry.

"Acidosis, you have written a complaint about Hercules?"

Acytosis snorted, another person saying his name wrong, "Acy-tosis is the correct way to say it, I am not an acid condition."

"The language of your complaint is very acidic, but as you wish. Tell me, at what specific point did you maintain a connection with Hercules?"

"Medulla Oblongata, of course. Very traditional, at the fight and flight response of the individual." Acytosis replied.

"Curious, Hercules doesn't appear to HAVE a flight response?"

"No, I removed it, to make more room. He didn't need it and I needed a more comfortable space in his brain."

"Do you still have it?" Ekatahuna was now interested.

But Acytosis was not, "I tossed it out ages ago," he lied.

Ekatahuna stared at him, as a vampire of Attachment, he knew his primal urge was at the base of all the other passions. "I can tell when you are lying to me, you know."

"How?" Acytosis protested.

"You moved your lips, now where is it?"

Acytosis looks miserable, "I put it in a jar, I suppose you want it?"

"I do. What do you want for it?"

"I am starving, I need a new host!" Acytosis responded. "And not a gerbil, I want a proper host, one with huge passions, someone who is worshipped."

Ekatahuna looked through the files, most decent hosts were fully booked, but here was an interesting one - a new project had enlarged the passion quotient and the fellow was positively brimming with excess emotion. "I got a good one for you. How about the Trumpetus Rex?"

Acytosis was practically salivating on the spot, "Yeah, that will do nicely, you want the flight response now?"

"Yes please," said Ekatahuna politely.

The Question

O rpheus stated the obvious when he asked, "The real question is WHY? Why does Vulcan want to end the world as we know it? If everything collapses what possible benefit would it be to him? He will no doubt survive, but to what purpose? Why is he ruining his OWN existence?"

Despite his enormous desire for excess, the Ogoglio was no fool. "I have known Vulcan for some time, run a few errands here and there, not a happy fellow. It may well be he doesn't like the way things are being run, and rather than put up with it, he prefers to be alone. Or maybe he just likes chaos?"

Orpheus scratched his chin, "Perhaps it has something to do with Hades, but what? I can't quite put my finger on it. If we knew the WHY of it, we would have a much better chance of sorting things."

Surprisingly, it was Brutus Maximus that laughed, saying, "Nonsense! What you need to know is the *why not* of it. When you have been around as long as Vulcan, your main question is "Why not?" He isn't interested in the Gods or Humans anymore, he just wants to beat metal into shape - it is the only thing he enjoys, so *why not* let everyone die?"

Orpheus is somewhat shocked, first that Hercules said something that sounded intelligent, and second because it made sense. "What excellent logic," he responded. "Why not, indeed?"

"And if we accept *why not* as the motivation, then next we must consider the consequence and ask: if not? And if not, why not if not?" Hercules said with a voice not quite his own.

Meridius snorted to Orpheus, "Oh, it sounds intelligent because it isn't Hercules. That would be a vampire then. Come on, show yourself!" she demanded.

Now, when the Oracle commands, which is a very rare thing, all of nature is compelled to obey. Despite their extremely long lives, Vampires are still creatures of nature and so Ekatahuna meekly stepped from the shadows of Hercules' brain, hopping out from the Medulla Oblongata and onto the shoulder of the Demi-God. He had to cover his eyes from the light of the goodness shining from Meridius, but at least he got to deliver the message. "I needed to convey a message because Vulcan is about to end all life as we know it and I could not approach you directly because of your angels," he whimpered.

"Mmmm," was all Meridius said.

"No, I am not his original haunting - that was a different vampire. I am in charge of administration and have been given the job of stopping Vulcan from killing the Gods and Humans," he explained.

"Mmmmm?" went Meridius again, with a motherly question mark.

"No I have no idea why Vulcan is doing what he is doing, but if he kills everything we are doomed as well, and we will all end up in boring Hades, so we have to stop him!" Ekatahuna had never been so honest in all his life, and surprisingly, it felt quite good. *OMG's* (Oh My Gods), he said to himself, for as he thought this he realized he DID feel GOOD! How very strange.

"Mmmmm," Meridius said in a less severe manner.

Ekatahuna had a tear in his eye, a thing he had not known he was capable of, "Thank you Oracle." and felt this shiver of goodness running down his vampire spine.

Meridius softened, "Now explain your question."

"Well, the *Why Not* is self-evident. He doesn't give a damn about anyone or anything. So *why not* trash the world, and see what happens next, because he is bored with it as it is? The NEXT question he will ask is *'If not?'* What happens if he doesn't? Well, it will be more of the same, which gives an added strength to the *'Why Not?'* But he checks with a further question, as the *'if not'* indicates he should end the world, he then asks, *'Why not If Not?'* Was there any reason at all why he should not trash the entire place? And if he cannot get a decent answer as to why he shouldn't this means he will. Do you see?"

Orpheus nodded seriously, "I do see. And we all know Vulcan, he is bad tempered enough to want us all gone. He will do it, Meridius - Now we know he will, we have to find a reason he won't."

Meridius sighed, "He has been on his own way too long. I should have understood him better, he just needed someone to love."

The Ogoglio laughs out loud, "Come now! Vulcan? In Love? That is crazy talk!"

"Hmmmm," replied Meridius

It was Ofal who replied, "He does want to be loved, you know. Everyone does, he is just very bad at asking for it. He is very shy, you see."

Rufus just looked at him, "And how the Hades do you know what Vulcan likes?"

Ofal shuffled his feet, "Oh, I used to help out on the bellows before I met you."

Rufus took matters in hand, only giving a sideways glance at the strange little fellow he convinced to form a troupe of unfunny comedians in a bar in Rome years ago. He vaguely remembered the explanation he gave Ofal of why they should, because he had protested saying he was not in the least bit funny, "That's the whole point, you aren't. But as we are unfunny comedians it is the perfect fit for you!"

He was still a bit surprised that Ofal joined him, but then he remembered he also offered free food and lodging in a donkey cart. "Look," he said with his most serious voice, "First we have to get there, talk with this Vulcan, and make him see sense. We won't sort anything out standing around here!"

He was surprised that anyone listened to him, but they all (bar Hercules, who was standing there looking fairly vacant with a sorry-looking vampire on his shoulder) nodded in agreement.

Dragons

Now, as this story is all about releasing the Dragon of Imagination, and how much damage this might cause, I feel a little background on Dragons might be necessary. Earlier we established they are not the long, winnowing things that people describe, but tend to be short, fat, and reasonably stupid. We have also established there are two types of dragon, Scaley and Feathery. Both love to sit on hordes of gold.

But there are 'other' dragons. These are very, very ancient creatures who look nothing like the modern ones. It is difficult to describe how they look, because they are largely invisible and if you DO happen to see one as it travels through an ion storm, they tend to get annoyed and go "Omph" in your direction, thus squashing you with a blast of pure dragon force.

Several points of interest to cover here: *Being made visible in Ion Storms,* or indeed any strong field of energy, is important - this tells us they love to bathe in pure energy. These ancient dragons are essentially just this, pure energy, and if you can see them at all they have a sort of rainbow sheen, not dissimilar to that oil-on-water appearance, but less oily. You can see right through them, yet the surface is almost visible, and when it appears, it is like an almost transparent shifting tide of liquid rainbow. Very easy to miss. But if they encounter a strong energy field, this phosphoresces about the dragon, and you can see them quite clearly.

This allows us to spot the odd one if they are about. One excellent example is when a dragon happens to wander past a wizard casting a particularly strong spell. In this instance, the energy of the spell will wrap around it for a moment and go "whhoooo" - some say the spell goes there because it feels it founds its mother, but I cannot say this is a certainty, only that the dragon glows briefly with the energy from it.

And it is a very happy sounding "Whoooo, in case you were wondering.

The other relevant point: There is no Fire Breathing with Ancient Dragons. Their breath doesn't burn anything, but some say it will change everything. This is difficult to prove because if everything has changed then we have lost our reference point as to what was before this. Some say dragon breath is the cause of all life and the instigator of the physical realm, but honestly, how would anyone know?

What we DO know is they are ancient, and I do mean ancient. We are not talking mere millennia here, but potentially a million years or more.

Here is the important thing, while they do not breathe fire, they give off an "Omph". This sounds trite, but the onomatopoeia is clear, the energy looks like an Omph, and sounds like this as well. They might look at you, and if you hear an "Omph", you will go "Oomph" yourself and then find yourself barreling backwards at a great rate of knots.

Some say this is a mating sound, and that you are SUPPOSED to go "Wumph" in return, and that the mighty exchange of energy between two ancient dragons is what produces new dragons, which are a combination of Omph and Wumph. But this is merely hearsay and I would dare to suggest that anyone claiming to know this for certain is lying. In this narrator's humble opinion, if you have been unlucky enough to experience an Omph, then I suspect that dealing with a combined interchange of Omph and Wumph would be somewhat life-ending, and so you would be giving your description from the grave.

Which, I will not deny, can be done via a suitable Vampire or Angel. But it is unlikely, because if you had an Angel it is extremely unlikely they would have allowed you to die so horribly, and if you had a vampire they wouldn't care and will have left you the moment you kicked it - so all your transcribing of events would be like a fart in the breeze, which someone might pick up downwind, but they won't like it.

Yes, I know, you protest and tell me that your story could be recorded in Hades and given to some God who was visiting, but have you forgotten? Gods have no memory, and supplies of writing paper in the underworld are in extremely short supply. It is not impossible, but it is not very likely.

The thing about Ancient Dragons is that their gold horde is exceedingly large, and came about because of their peculiar habit of collecting pretty much anything. Yet the VALUE to the Dragon is not for its human worth, but in the aura the object carries. They are strange and curious creatures who look at something someone might have cast aside and wonder about the story behind it. You see, stories are the only thing these really old dragons value. A good story is better than anything else, and if you happen to be able to peel off a good one, you will have made a friend for life.

The other thing ancient dragons love, besides scrabble, is a good riddle. If you can combine a riddle with a story, well you will become an instant favorite. This is why Morpheus was on such good terms with one ancient dragon called Sihorne' and it is also why he lived such a long life, for when an ancient dragon breathes his kindness over you, it is effectively the gift of immortality.

Now, I presume you are not foolish and are presently asking how can an Ancient Dragon turn junk into a horde of gold? Indeed, this is a sensible question, and the answer is called recycling. You see, dragons love peculiar things because of their story, but a peculiar habit of humans is that when they see that someone values something, they want it. You may say, "But it is only junk!" Well, my friend, junk is only junk when it is cast out into the street - it has the backdrop of being unloved, and the average human will say, "Pfft, unloved rubbish!" and walk straight on by.

But put that same rubbish on a shelf in a recycling depot, with a hefty price tag on it, and humans go, "Ohhh, now THAT is interesting!" Subsequently, they love to haggle, and so the Ancient Dragon always puts a higher price on his beautiful junk than what it is worth.

It possibly explains why they have let humans live because while humans financially support their recycling centers, they also create enormous piles of fascinating things that they throw away, ignoring the beautiful story attached to them.

Why one human would throw away an old and ruined ox cart wheel, and another would pay gold to buy it from a dragon junkyard, who can say? But what we CAN say is that very few humans were prepared to risk life and limb to buy directly off a dragon. No, you need an intermediary which is why the Ancient Dragons became very good employers of humans, for in the dim distant stone age, certain storyteller cavemen got on well with their resident dragon, and so they were granted very long lives. As a byproduct of this friendship, they also found useful and very long-term employment trading things from the local dragon horde.

This also explains why the men running recycling yards look a lot like Neanderthals.

These appointments have meant that fathers employ their children, and so on for generations. But, as is the way, when things are not specifically written down, by the seventh or eighth generation, the people working in and running the recycling centers forget they work for a dragon. Nor are they generally aware that they work for a pittance, seeing as the dragon had no reason to pay them any more than he had ever done, despite the cost of living increases.

Nor could they find a fair comparison of wages from people who worked at other recycling centers, because they too were working for an Ancient Dragon. As a result of these low wages and the human need to constantly buy junk, these ancient dragons became incredibly wealthy, and the gold coins just kept pouring in the door.

Here is the thing, given that the workers forgot they worked for a dragon, you might have thought with all that gold about, they would have been tempted to take some. But no, while they may not have been CONSCIOUSLY aware of the dragon, it still looked at them through the eyes of the semi-immortal Neanderthal supervisor. No words were said, but everyone knew, no matter how high that pile of gold in the middle of the scrap yard grew, don't even THINK of taking one for yourself.

As a complete side note, a thing not relative to the story, there was another tribe of Neanderthals that went missing. These were called the Meanderthals, and where they meandered, no one knows.

And while we are on sidebars not relevant to the story, I must come clean and admit - this narrator did do an extraordinarily stupid thing one day. I was in one of these scrap yards and I asked a fellow who had some second-hand gym equipment that someone had thrown out what it was worth. The price seemed fair, and somehow I got to ask him about how much people earned in these places, at which point the man immediately became evasive, like I was touching on a forbidden subject.

So I tried to draw a comparison, saying, "Well, I have a friend who works in a different sort of scrap yard, he sells junk bonds, and makes One Thirty Talents a year ."

The fellow's face paled, as he whispered, "I only get ten talents a year!"

Not very talented, as the old quip goes. But as soon as he said this, the supervisor looked directly at me with an unearthly gaze, one that I knew instantly to be that of a dragon. Wisely, I snipped the conversation short, paid my tithe by buying the gym equipment I will never use, and left. To make sure I was not followed, I dropped the said gym equipment at the nearest curb, knowing that this would throw the dragon off my scent. Apparently, it worked, for I am still here.

And if you think I was foolish, or perhaps paranoid, well consider - what was going to happen to the gym equipment anyway? I would have looked at it guiltily for three years, then tossed it onto the curb. So, I saved myself three years of recrimination and a whole lot of effort carting it home. And when you think about it, the only exercise anyone who buys gym equipment ever gets is found in the effort of taking it home and subsequently throwing it out.

This is what makes it valuable to Ancient Dragons, because of all the stories of frustration and poor discipline that go with it. I was not there, but I can imagine some worker doing kerbside scavenging came across the gym equipment I tossed aside in fear, and took it to his supervisor, who smelled the story and took THAT to his dragon, who sniffed it and said, "Worth $200!"

Now we are up to date with Ancient Dragons, of which the Dragon of Imagination was one, I need to point out one salient point. All the Ancient Dragons I knew of were not 'of' anything. You might think there was a Dragon of Inspiration, but no, that job was taken by the Muses. Perhaps you might hope to find a Dragon of Perspiration, but that job was given to the peasants. Maybe these things existed in the far distant past, but it seems in the present day that whatever a dragon was 'of' was no longer important.

Some say they were born in a long-dead civilization on some other planet and flew here for the nice things that were being tossed out by humans. Others say the dragons were here before the planet was formed, and they had gathered up asteroids and put them all into one spot, which is how planets were created, and that it was the Dragon of Imagination who ruled them all.

Some say that all the noble ideals of man were forged by that specific dragon in the fires of our sun, and beaten into the atoms of consciousness that would one day awaken as the human race, and that when the Gods came to earth they captured it and put it into an egg. Who can say? The Gods have no memory and the other ancient dragons are too busy running recycling centers.

No, what the Gods think about are questions like: *Could Hercules beat an ancient dragon?* They know, only because it was recorded, that a batch of them had to work to house one dragon and put it into an egg, but no one recorded exactly how it was done. In the library of epic battles, which is at Mount Olympus, there is no quibbling insignificance about *"he did this"* or *"she did that"* but more, *"the mighty power of Zeus conquered"* or *"an epic battle of vast proportions was won"*. Gods are BIG, they only record BIG things, not insignificant minutia or tiny human things like accurate history.

But they DO wonder about certain things, and one of them is the postulate of what happens when the unstoppable warrior meets the immovable dragon. You might think this is a very strange thing to ponder because dragons are eminently moveable, so we can presume they really mean is, *"Can anyone move an Ancient Dragon off its horde?"*. As it stood, present events were quite possibly about to offer an answer to this riddle.

However, before we get to this final Armageddon, there is a different question to ask, which is: *How come Hercules is so strong and unable to be defeated?*

The answer may surprise you, certainly, there is an aura of Godhood about him, which certainly helps, but really, it is in the attitude. To explain: Gods do not care much about anything. Despite all those people praying to them for this and that, as long as they get their faith energy, the rest doesn't matter. How this affects strength is obvious, for if you go into the back garden to have a pee (and girls DO pee in their backyards as well, but for the purpose of this allegory, we will make it only guys) and a lizard is staring at you, what do you care? You can pee away as lord and ruler of the backyard, which you are.

But if an amazingly beautiful woman is there, looking at you, you can't! You are no longer lord and ruler, you are a sniveling wreck of a man, wanting her to think well of you, but extremely conscious that she may look and go, "oh dear". You become INTROVERTED, fearful, weak - in short, the exact opposite of Hercules. If he saw a beautiful woman in the backyard looking at him, he would presume she must be a serving wench and demand more beer.

Here is the secret: Power comes from not giving a rats. By not even considering the possibility you could lose, you can't. It is a very simple psychology. If you DO happen to land a blow on Hercules, he laughs, thinking it is a great sport, and clubs you back in a friendly fashion, as if to say, "Great game!".

So, I know you are dying to ask this question: *What happens when an Ancient Dragon goes "Omph" towards Hercules?* Well, as yet, no one knows. But I assure you, at some point, I expect we will find out.

The question I have is far more serious, for if the Dragon of Imagination got unleashed, and the predictions of Ekatahuna were proven true, how does this affect the Ancient Dragons? After all, their business is recycling, but if people can just imagine whatever they want, they will have no need to go to a recycling yard and buy things they think they want. No, they can stay home and just mock them up before throwing them out.

On the surface, it would seem like heaven for the recycling collectors - bigger and better things would be thrown out every day, yet there would be no real story to them. Plus, though their yards were full to the brim, no customers would turn up thus no gold would be put onto the horde.

It seems to me that if you have all the imagination in the world to create whatever you want, then all struggle and effort is gone. It is like the rich musician who had a string of hits, they keep churning out the songs like they did in their heyday but the STORY behind them is now facile and weak. Would a dragon sniff a song from a 1980s musician and, sensing the lack of story, even want it? I suspect not. The result off too much imagination and no story will be that all the sidewalk junk will just sit there, rusting away.

But wind forward a year: *What happens when everyone starts dying?* We all know how those great beasts think, it is all about the stories. So what happens when the people start dying and the stories come to an end? Logically, as the stories are based on people having some sort of event, the dragons need us, they NEED people and events, as they lead to more stories.

And so to the calamitous end predicted by Ekatahuna, where the Ancient Dragon of Imagination is left to run rife and mankind dies out, along with the gods, along with the stories. The question is this: *Will the lessening of stories in recycling centers cause the other Ancient Dragons to act?* Is it possible they will so something to save us before it is all destroyed? I just do not know. What I suspect is they might just see it as a sort of close of business and move to another planet. (Good luck to them finding something akin to humans with their insane desire to buy junk, however.)

Even so, at this very moment, nothing is set in stone. The pen having writ, moves on, and all of that. It is time for the pen to write the story so we can, at last, get to the start of the God Games.

Pumpkin Fudge

There was a great hubbub surrounding the start of the God Games, as everyone called them. For one, people fully expected to see Gods, thus proving all those ridiculous atheists wrong. This is a thing, dear reader - we have grown accustomed to a close and intimate view of Gods and how they think, or don't think, as the case may be - but the vast majority of the population have no such connection.

The ordinary man in the street has a life that is, as the name suggests, ordinary. This is to say, nothing extraordinary ever occurs for him. Most believe their lives to be dull, an experience lacking in spice or even a modicum of interest. Ask the ordinary man in the street what he did yesterday and he will answer with words that say, "More of what I did the day before that!" This is the very definition of ordinary, to do the same thing today that you did yesterday.

However, a paradox. The Gods, as a rule, are fairly ordinary. Their lives are predictable and humdrum, just as ours might be. After you have thrown your thirty-thousandth thunderbolt, throwing yet another one is mundane stuff. Yes, it was extraordinary at the start, but repetition makes us all ordinary.

This is why television hosts do anything and everything so as not to appear ordinary. Ordinary, to the ordinary man, is something entirely undesirable that must be avoided at any cost - and indeed, the cost of not being ordinary is exceptionally high. You need the best house, the most expensive cart, and the largest block of land on the highest point in the most fashionable city to not be ordinary and the very fact that this is far out of reach of the ordinary man simply proves it.

This is why TV is glossed over with fantastic looking objects that are for sale. It is a certainty these things that are the real attraction, the reason all the denizens of the Earth tune in every day. It is to look at these objects d'art. Of course, some fools think TV is about the programs, the dramas, the melodramas, and the not-very-funny comedies that mindlessly absorb your attention - but no! It is the advertisements everyone gets excited over.

You only have to sit in any household to see the proof of this. As soon as advertisements come on the populace gets very excited, they jump up, run to the fridge, or run to the bathroom, because they cannot contain their enthusiasm. But coming back to the present, the TV presenters were trying to find something interesting to say about the Tour De Gaul, which was about to begin.

The problem with talking about a bicycle race that will go on for over three weeks, there is very little to say. There's no actual drama until someone gets squashed by a God-thrown rock, and there is no storyline. I mean, seriously, all you do is follow a bunch of people on bikes up and down hills. If it were not for the possibility of some God Action, it would not have been screened at all.

Even then, Gods are invisible to mortal eyes. All you get to see is the evidence of Gods throwing rocks, etc. but the cynics just proclaim this to be a landslide, or similar. Worse, if the defending Gods are winning, you don't even get to see the odd bicyclist squished. So the journalists did what they always do, find something to talk about to fill in the empty spaces between the lack of action.

There are three presenters for the morning show, all are tanned and blonde, fit and healthy, and good-looking. We all know that to be on TV you have to be in the top 5% of looks. The one that opens the show is John Johnny Johns, or JJJ to his friends (which happened to be the entire viewing audience) and he perks up with, "Hey, I recently discovered that Americans call pumpkin mash Pumpkin FUDGE?"

"Really?" asks Suzy so so Suez, or SSSS to her friends, which was also the entire viewing audience.

"Noooo!" exclaims Patty Pat Pat (called, yes PPP to her friends). "That's just crazy! I have never heard such a wild out-there thing!"

JJJ crosses to a Professor from Americanus, "This is Professor Bilge from Columbia State. Professor, why do you Americans call Pumpkin mash Pumpkin Fudge? Is it because you add sugar? I know you Americans love lots of sugar."

Professor Bilge looks down the camera, tilts his glasses forward to peer over them, and says, "Well JJJ, SSSS, and PPP, I am not sure this is correct. Pumpkin mash is mashed pumpkin, and pumpkin fudge is a fudge made using pumpkins."

PPP interjects, "So it IS the sugar then, that is what makes the difference? I can't see what difference would be between your FUDGE and ordinary pumpkin pie, other than there is no pastry - so we could call your Pumpkin Fudge a pastry-less pumpkin pie, yes Professor?"

The good professor is looking very confused, "Ah, PPP - I don't think pumpkin pie is the same as pumpkin fudge..."

To which SSSS adds, "That's correct Professor - because it has no pastry, that's right, isn't it?" she demands.

Seeing the professor is a little lost for words, JJJ steps in, "Fantastic SSSS. That is the sort of clarity that explains everything. Thank you Professor for your insight and wisdom."

The good professor is snipped from the screen, looking about his home in Upstate New Rome, saying to his wife, "What the ... ?"

At that moment the ads start to roll, and the three presenters all pull out cigarettes and have a smoke, talking as they always do about the screen impact of the last guest. "He didn't have the IT factor," PPP expounded.

"I agree," adds SSSS. "Next time, let's try to get someone with a little more onscreen persona."

At which point JJJ had to pass on the latest bit of gossip, "Hey, I don't think we can send this to air, but did you hear about Zeus?"

PPP is all ears, she had always had a bit of a fantasy about being taken away on the flying Pegasus. "No, tell us... what is the gossip?"

"Well," JJJ moves forward conspiratorially, "apparently he and LOKI have a thing going on. Yes lovems, bad boy Zeus is a GAY BOY, can you believe it?"

The girls gasped, this was sensational stuff, much better than the dreary professor - only there was a small problem, some technician had kept the cameras rolling and their words went out live for all to see - including Zeus.

He was packing up to go throw some rocks at cyclists and was about to mount his eagle. He had been watching the telecast for a few clues on who to squash first when news of him being GAY was leaked. You can imagine his fury at such character assassination. Instead of rocks, he started throwing thunderbolts at the TV studio where the unfortunate hosts were chatting.

Well, NOW thing got interesting. The Tour De Gaul had been a bit of a flop, but this is what the producers needed to pick up eyeballs. Great blasts of electricity turning TV presenters into toast was a thing of joy for them. Now millions started tuning in, looking to see what next exciting installment was in store with the bicycle race!

Bookmakers

There is a truth that has never failed mankind, gambling. Let's face it, we are even called the Human Race! We were DESIGNED to gamble on who would win. No matter what we do as a race, no matter where we go, we will find something to bet on. Always it has been our succor and joy to bet that your fly will land on that beer before that other person's fly. Gambling is the only true religion of the Roman Republic and despite all the Gods and all the temples, the real worshipping is done at the chariot races on Saturday.

Go there and discover the passion and happiness gambling brings. People are shouting with excitement, buying huge quantities of beer to share with friends, and for a brief few moments, these individuals experience an extraordinary release from the deep depression of everyday life. Hope and joy are the gifts gambling brings. Yes, a foolish hope and a temporary joy, but at least you get to experience some wonderful emotions beyond the beige sameness that is your life outside the racecourse.

The reason people like gambling as a religion is that the donations you must make are reasonable, and if you do this, you are in line for a HUGE return. What religion asks for money, then gives you a chance to not just get it back but to double and triple your money? Only gambling offers this sort of freedom and satisfaction.

The high priests of gambling are called Bookmakers. The golden rule of gambling; always trust the instincts of Bookmakers. They are the ones who calculate the sacred odds and bless you with their wisdom by exchanging a small ticket in return for your trust and devotion. This devotion comes in the form of gold or whatever is worth something to the bookmaker.

Every schoolboy knows the peasants pick their children up with a donkey, the middle classes collect their children with a horse and cart, the upper classes send the slaves down to piggyback them home, but the BOOKMAKERS, they collect their children with gilded coaches made by Mr. Rolls and Mr. Royce and drawn by magnificent stallions. Yes, they may be ex-racehorses they picked up cheap, but they still look magnificent.

When you consider what the other priests have on offer compared to the Bookmakers, it is in short, sweet butt all. What does the Temple of Juno exchange in return for your gold you lovingly place there? A prayer for your Soul! How pathetic - No, the bookmakers offer far more and you quickly come to appreciate the care and concern that they have for your money. They will cherish it, and give it a wonderful home, so you can be certain as you hand it over that it is all going towards a good cause. Plus, you stand a chance to collect more than you give them.

Well, I say "stand a chance" in a rhetorical sense. Yes, we all have a chance to get our money back, but we also know the truth is that all the bookmakers calculate their odds in such a way as to make this far less likely than what you believe. But that is not the important part, what matters is that for a few brief moments as you watch your chariot come around the bend, you can dream of winning. It warms the heart and gives a deep purpose to your day. As that chariot comes down the main straight looking like it has a chance, you feel the inflated sense of purpose and driven will to succeed that is akin to being a GOD!

You lose, because the race was rigged and your charioteer was paid to make sure he did no better than second, and afterward you get the withdrawal and suffering all proper addicts achieve in the post-adrenalin high, and now you feel like a DOG - But apart from the aftermath, that bricf moment was worth every penny you invested to experience the thrill of the chase.

Best of all is the "Sure Bet". This is supposedly the unlosable bid you make in the pursuit of happiness and the great goal of beating the odds. It is no coincidence that 'beating the odds" sounds an awful lot like beating the GODS, because to beat the Gods (or the bookmakers) you have about the same odds as a leaf beating the teeth of the goat that wants to eat it. This is not the point, you know you are going to lose, but the thrill and excitement of possibly winning make all your misery and strife disappear for a brief few moments.

The term "Sure Bet" came from a Phoenician trader, back in the early days of the Republic, when Caesar hired him to run a galley past some pirates that he wished the trap. When I say "hire" I mean he brought some war triremes up beside the fellow and instructed him to do this. When the fellow protested saying it was suicide Caesar blithely assured him it was if he didn't do it THAT was suicide. However he accepted that there was a risk of the fellow losing his cargo, so perhaps he would like to deposit it with Caesar for safekeeping?

To which the Phonecian replied, "I thought you were supposed to be catching pirates, not imitating them?" Caesar laughed, encouraged by the man's spirit, and asked what his cargo might be. The captain explained it was a concoction very popular in the East called 'Sherbert'. This is the thing, because of the fellow's thick accent, it sounded like "Sure Bet".

"So what is this Sure bet, and what does it do?" Caesar asked the man.

Now because of Caesar's clipped, impersonal attitude and the very sharp sword by his side, the Phonecian did not correct the translation, and answered, "It is a mixture of sugar, gelatin, citric acid, a sprinkle of baking soda, and a white powder called Cocaine. You sniff it and aside from the wonderful tingling sensation in the nose, you now believe you are a God. You are embraced by the sensation that all is possible and that you cannot be beaten."

As we all know, after a few snorts of Sherbert, Caesar rounded up all the pirates, beat impossible odds, and achieved Godhood. So, if something was a "Sure Bet" it was seen as if you were betting on Caesar himself, which was a sure bet.

How much of Sherbert went up Caesar's nose and how responsible it was for his impossible conquests, we may never know, but the term itself came down to us as a sure sign that you were backing a winner.

Of course, as far as bookmakers went, the term "Sure bet" had an entirely different meaning. This was a rumor that you spread around that encouraged the punters to bet on something guaranteed to LOSE. It is the main reason they were so rich.

Right now, the "Sure Bet" was proving difficult to pin down. Most presumed it was Mars that would carry the day in the god Games, but there was that rather talented outsider from India called Shiva, and the Aztecs were supposed to be represented by a large Ancient Dragon called Quetzalcoatl. Thor was also a front-runner, but in defining exactly who the Sure Bet was going to be the bookmakers came across a seemingly insurmountable problem, how do you bribe a God?

And dammit, there were just so many of them. Instead of picking a single winner, the odds came down to imagined battles between Zeus and Odin, Mars versus Thor, etc. Or they became fanciful notions such as Athena versus the Amazons. In all these things odds were given, yet it was entirely uncertain if any such battle would ever take place. The problem was that trying to get a defined list of events out of the Gods was an impossibility.

In the end, the bookmakers slapped their foreheads and finally understood what the games were about, parochialism! All they had to do was run separate lists in every country putting the Gods of THAT culture up as the Sure Bet. It was a certainty that the Vikings would place bets on Thor or Odin, just as it was certain the Romans would place their bets on Zeus or Mars.

But this was not the brilliancy of the bookmaker's plan - it was in making the bets about the bets themselves! Sure the bookmakers could put up the theoretical shot-put battle between Vulcan and Atlas, but we know this will probably never happen. I mean, who would hold up the world during the contest?

As it could not be certain the Gods would even come to blows in the way they had predicted, the only TRUE certainty is that the winner could never be known. It was not a chariot race, held in one spot, where simple bribes could determine the winner - no this was a far more ethereal contest where winning and losing were difficult to quantify. Herein lay the sheer brilliancy of the Bookmakers plan - The WINNER of this contest was not the so called contest, it would be the people who bet the MOST for a particular God.

In the Zeus versus Odin fight, the winner would be the God who got the most bets. Simple! In this way, the bookmakers pitted Vikings against Romans, Greek against Indians, one nationality versus another, and in every town the "Sure Bet" was always THEIR God. And here was the sheer beauty of the whole thing, the bookies would tell the Indians the Greeks won, but tell the Greeks that the Indians won.

Yes, there would be a small payout to those stubborn, irascible betters who insisted on betting against the odds, but this would be nothing in comparison to the rake.

However, in the middle of the flurry of betting, Zeus let loose a lightning bolt that killed a whole set of TV presenters. What were the odds of THAT? Suddenly the bookmakers were confronted by a real and dangerous possibility that the Gods might become involved, which would be the Gods versus the Bookmakers.

Now THAT is an intriguing thing to place a bet on!

The betting opened with the Bookmakers as odds-on favorites. How could this be so, you ask? How could mere humans beat the Gods? It is very simple, should the Bookmakers lose, if they make themselves the Sure Bet they will have a whole lot of extra money to help them run away to a deserted island. This is known as the "each way" bet - no matter what happens, they cannot lose.

"Oh HO!" you cry out, "But what if the people are smart and bet on the GODS to win? The bookmakers will have to pay out a massive loss to the punters, who will finally win the day."

How foolish of you. Even if you could find one of the bookmakers to claim your bet, even if you went to that far distant island, what do you think will happen? You will hold up your chit that says he owes you one million denarius and he will just laugh, saying, "Sorry, bankrupt, because I lost!" This is the eternal Catch-22 of the Bookmakers - the odds are ever in their favor.

Game On

The Tour De Gaul had started, with the Augustus team versus the Caesar team, away on their bicycles up the hills and down the valleys, all racing towards Paris. The Gods were hurtling rocks at them, while other gods were batting them off as the humans ducked the lumps and bumps created in the road by the argument above them.

A new set of presenters had been moved in, warned about not saying anything about Gay Boy Zeus. As TV people do, they prattled on as if something interesting were happening. Yet, predictably, when they were off-screen, Gay Boy Zeus was all they talked about. "Well, he IS Greek after all," one of them started to say.

But equally as predictable, the techs left THAT camera running as well, because the truth is, ratings were hard to get while TV presenters were a dime a dozen. Another barrage of lightning ensued the next set of presenters knew not to say anything even remotely gossipy about Zeus. Oh, but they wanted to - how much they wanted to, yet even at the urgings of the rating officer in the studio, they knew better.

None of this was observed by the Oracle or her party as they were already on the way to see Vulcan. After the vampire called Ekatahuna turned up and explained what was happening, Meridius decided they needed to act and summoned a few of the Pegasus to get them there quickly. And as to your secret question about whether she had read the thoughts of Rufus wondering why they had to sail all the way to Greece when they could have caught a flying horse, we may never know, but you can be assured that Rufus DID think this and that most probably you would not need to be a psychic to read those thoughts.

The fact is, our dear Oracle was well loved by all BECAUSE she never abused her rights and privileges. Few understand this sort of economy. You take the average person and put them in a first class carriage, and the first thing they think is, "Oh I am in first class, I wonder what the peasants are doing behind me in ECONOMY?" Economy quickly becomes a word meaning poverty and as such represents a thing that must be avoided.

Splashing money about like a toddler in a bath is what most of the nouveau rich do, but the Gods find that dull. They are used to being wealthy and having whatever they want, yet they are also surprisingly economical. Yes, some say golden goblets are an extravagance, and fonts of ambrosia an excess, and perhaps the small mountains of seafood for lunch are a tad over the top, but what Gods want to see when they look down on creation is appreciation, and being economical is one way of saying you appreciate their gifts.

So while they don't care about money or things (they are Gods, after all) they DO care if you show respect. Once you demonstrate a little respect, then using the odd Pegasus for a lift in emergencies is seen as being perfectly reasonable. Adding a chariot to this to make it possible to take along a batch of people, well that IS downright economical in the purest sense of the word.

It does tend to mean you cannot sneak up, however. If secrecy is your thing, you are far better off taking one of the huge Eagles from Mount Olympus, but in this case, they were all booked for the Tour de Gaul games - They were far more impressive than horses plus they can hold large rocks in their talons. On top of this, they are a much better thing to be seen on when legends are going to be written about you - for it was a Sure Bet that not one of the Gods imagined that legends were NOT going to be written about them - So, for the game, eagles it had to be.

Did I hear someone ask about unicorns? Are you mad?

What no one in their right mind takes out for a quiet trip are Unicorns. We have covered this in the last book, but these h-ornery (pun intended) and facile creatures are the devil's own children. They are evil tempered, highly-strung creatures that are as likely to attack their rider as the person foolishly walking across the street in front of them. It is VERY unwise to have anything at all to do with unicorns, and it is very much hoped they do not make an appearance in this book.

When the chariot clattered down at Mount Vesuvius, making a significant rattling as the metal hooves of the flying horses scraped over the stone, Vulcan appeared not to notice. He was busy over his forge, cursing and swearing like a trooper as he hammered away at whatever it was. More importantly, beside him sat a rather sweet feathered dragon who would occasionally oblige a puff of dragon breath. The important part is that the little dragon sat on a large egg - the Omphalos.

Vulcan was cursing away at such an extraordinary rate that even Rufus, very used to many curse words being thrown at him by the public, had to ask, "Why does he curse all the time? Doesn't he like what he is doing?"

The Ogoglio answered, "Foolish boy, if you are going to make weapons for the gods, curses are necessary. The louder and more colorful the curse, the better the steel. The saying is that bad temper tempers better. But evil temper, and do not doubt this is the case with Vulcan, tempers best."

And Vulcan was letting fly with the cursing, "You miserable low-life cur of a pathetic dog!" he shouted at the metal as he beat it. "Filthy little snidey bunt unworthy of being called scum!" There were many other fierce and dangerous words he uttered as he bashed away at the red-hot steel, but I fear these would offend your ears. However, you get the picture.

The swearing was SO loud and abusive that even Hercules was impressed, but not so with Meridius. She just went right up to where he was working, and went, "Mmmmm."

Vulcan gave her a sideways glance and was about to go back to beating and swearing the hot metal, but he found the words just wouldn't come. So he went to the next level and started MUTTERING.

The Ogoglio held his breath, "OMG, he is MUTTERING - this means he is getting very serious about making super god weapons!" The fact that the Ogoglio was getting excited seemed to spur Vulcan on!

He lifted his hammer, mumbling, "whhhen whhe nuuun whazza whhus mutter mutter mutter," as he slammed the hammer down with such force the very mountain itself started to ring. He then indicated for Myrtle to puff some heat into the furnace, but she just looked at him, then looked at Meridius, then looked back at him, then looked at Meridius, until Vulcan gave up, put the hammer down, and demanded, "Well, what?"

Meridius didn't even fold her arms, just looked at him. "Mmmmm?" she asked.

"They have been here long enough," he bellowed back.

Enough was enough, Meridius didn't just fold her arms, she pursed her lips and stared right back at him.

Vulcan was shocked and took a step back. The Ogoglio was amazed, exclaiming, "She didn't just fold her arms, she PURSED her LIPS at him! I cannot even recall a time when she was THIS angry."

Vulcan went to say something, but Meridius took it to the next level, she raised one eyebrow and firmly put her finger to her lips, and went, "Shhhh!"

That was it, the God of Volcanoes could take no more - he dropped his hammer and started to cry. "I am sorry," he blubbered, "But they are very rude, and they never pay for their weapons, and they NEVER say thank you, or give me credit for the work I do. I have a right to want them all dead. Even if I don't care how rude they are, they still need to be reminded that a little courtesy goes a long way."

Meridius just looked down her long nose, and went, "Mmmmmm."

Vulcan, of course, knew what she meant. The truth was, the most discourteous of all the Gods was himself, but he explained, "I have to be rude - it is part of the persona, and it means I can make better weapons. You heard what I have to do, I have to beat curses into them, to make them better."

Meridius just shook her head.

"Well, OK - maybe that is a little lie I told everyone because I like to swear, but it seems to work," he answered, not knowing why he was feeling so defensive.

And then it happened! Right at this point, the Omphalos cracked, and out popped a rather magnificent little dragon. She was cute as a button, in that ancient invisible dragon sort of way, and if you looked at the happy phosphorescence you could see a divine little smile in there.

Even Vulcan was charmed, "Awww, isn't she a sweety!"

The invisible ball of energy floated over to where Meridius was, and brushed her invisible head against Meridius, looking for a snack, no doubt. Myrtle the dragon clucked with delight, and went over to smooth down the ruffled fur of her newborn - you have to presume that dragons could see invisible things - and clucked and cooed all over the little darling.

Orpheus was the one who spoke up, "We cannot let ourselves be charmed by this sweet little dragon," he explained, and even as he said it, he was all doe-eyed at just how CUTE she was.

"I agree," said the Ogoglio, as he too cooed and clucked over the wonderful little cuddly thing.

Ofal was off with the fairies, looking like he had fallen in love, and Rufus stood there, amazed. "By the GODS!" he exclaimed, "Don't you see this dragon is here to end the entire world? What can we DO about it?"

At that particular point, Hercules went over and was looking at the sword Vulcan was making, apparently entirely unaware of the existence of the Dragon of Imagination. "Fine blade Vulcan old boy!" he exclaimed in his usual boisterous voice that had enthusiasm for everything that was a weapon.

Now, if you understand Ancient Dragons, you know they are very much like cats. Some say that cats (not chickens) are the result of Ancient Dragon farts, but I cannot be certain of this - however, they do share traits, the first being curiosity, and the second being they are fascinated by anyone who ignores them. Because of this, she wanted to get the attention of this enigmatic soul who paid her no attention. Brutus Maximus had no interest in dragons, just in swords, and in particular

THIS sword. It reminded him an awful lot of the one he gave away to Authur. He had always regretted selling it.

Here I will tax your memory. Remember way back when we asked what would happen if a dragon "omph" bumped into Hercules? Well, turns out it wasn't the immovable object meeting the unstoppable one, nothing like that at all.

The real question became: What can fascinate fascination? Ancient Dragons are fascination itself, yet as Hercules was utterly entranced by the magnificent sword just made by Vulcan, this fascination was stronger than the Dragon Mystique. This meant the little dragon forgot everyone and everything else and became fascinated by the fascination. She went right up to the Demi-God and purred and cooed and demanded attention.

When Rupus Murdochius ran up to get a wish fulfilled, the dragon did not even see him. When the Trumpetus Rex shouted to the dragon that he had some gold for it to sit on, it ignored him. It only had eyes for Brutus Maximus.

Finally, Merlin was able to throw off the anti-magic net because he realized that just because he can't use magic to remove it, he COULD use his hands. All he had to do was lift it off. Now he was free of impediment, he was lifting his wand to cast a powerful spell to stop time and repair all the damage when he realizes, Meridius is there and has taken charge of everything. She just looks at him, standing there ready to cast a spell with the wand. "But the Dragon of Imagination has been released!" he exclaims, wondering why everyone seemed so calm.

However, his words were said with his wand raised, so it formed a powerful incantation - one that spread into the atmosphere and was heard by the Gods as they were throwing rocks down on the helpless humans in the Tour de Gaul. When they all heard was *'the Dragon of Imagination has been released '*, they immediately stopped with the rocks and put their attention onto what Vulcan was doing. They saw the cracked Omphalos and remembered (at last) that this was a more significant problem than most they ignored.

But Meridius was there, so it should be OK.

Even so, the game seemed to lose their interest and they stopped throwing rocks, which meant the ones stopping the rocks had nothing to stop, so they stopped stopping things and everyone pretty much headed home.

Only the Christian God remained on the scene. He hadn't noticed the changing of events because he was looking at the demon-graphics of the new slogan, "Odin Saves!" He looked at the Holy Spirit, then at Jesus, and asked, "So this increases market share?"

"It does," says Jesus, enthusiastically. "We estimate well over 50% before the end of the decade."

"Hmmmm," Jehovah said, "I always thought it would be a deal with the Romans to get us across the line, but if it is to be the Vikings, I am good with that."

"Ah," said Jesus apologetically, "it does have a few conditions, as in, no more destructions of whole cities and you have got to let promiscuity be allowed."

"Well, I don't know about that..." Jehovah was doubtful.

It was the Ghosty who spoke up, in that whispering wind-like voice it had, "But not AFTER marriage, before is acceptable, but not AFTER?"

Jesus smiled, "That should work," he said, not telling them about the divorce clause or the fact that once they ticked this off they were OUT, replaced by the Nordic Gods. But he kept them believing he was doing just what they wanted because it was precisely what he had planned to do anyway. Everyone knows, nothing sells better with humans than telling them they can't have it, and that what you are selling is forbidden. Every bondage mistress knows this and they are held in high regard by Jehovah.

Which of course presents a philosophical musing, that if Jehovah is the highest of the Gods, how can he be overthrown? Surely, the best you could do is to underwhelm him? The truth was the old God was an underperformer and like any player on a football team who did not meet the mark, that cantankerous hater of Egyptians deserved to be pushed aside.

Werewolves

Foolishly, I had thought, or at least hoped, that this was the end of this tale. As a recorder of events, I am paid per job, not by the hour, and honestly, not paid very well. I had pretty much packed up my quill and ink, rolled up my scroll, and was about to head home when I heard the baying of the werewolves descending on the hapless humans still struggling up hills and across valleys with their silly race.

And I have to admit, I wanted to walk away and ignore the fact they were about to all get eaten because to tell you the truth, the notion of making yourself suffer so you can wear a yellow jersey seemed so utterly pointless to me that part of me WANTED them all to die. My motto echoes the famous New Rome Jewess, Ruby Radner. When she was asked about fitness, her answer was a truth for the ages: "They say: No pain, no gain. I say: No pain, no pain!" she said, enunciating the pure undefiled message of indulgence over good looks.

But in a remarkable coincidence, the place where the riders in the Tour De Gaul were to stay overnight was the same town where the cult of the Fox Hat was based. Knowing that all these potential purchasers were coming through, the dwarves had teamed up with the cult members. They had spent the last week selling the Fox Fur Hat cult on the magnificent opportunities presented by trading their hats via Multi-Level Marketing.

As each rider pulled in, a HUGE banner welcomed them, carrying the adjusted motto of the Games, "Let them HAT it!" Yes, the mistaken motto had found its way onto a huge banner and when the people on the bicycles came into town they found a dwarf pulling them to one side, saying, "Have I got a deal for you!" as they held up a delightful fox-fur hat. Now, you may well ask yourself, what on earth would a sweaty, exhausted bicycle rider who had just struggled over tens of miles of hills and dales want with a fur hat - the obvious answer is, they don't. But never underestimate the persuasive nature of a dwarf in full flight!

As the poor fellows were too exhausted to ride away, the dwarves cleverly provided fluids and a free place to stay the night, as long as they signed up to be a distributor of the fur hats, and as long as they wore the same about town (which is the essence of all good business, free advertising). Well, most of the riders were so tired after ducking rocks and other riders with slingshots, that they signed the form, and took a hat, without even realizing they had also signed up as perpetual stockists and resellers of Shamway.

Yes, the Fox Fur Hat had found its way into the greatest multi-level marketing scheme of all time, and became one of its leading lines. Shamway represented an incredible opportunity for wealth and happiness, where, by sharing your list of friends, you too can capitalize on their gullibility and profit from them. Forget social media, forget influencers, dwarves were the driving force of one of the greatest powers on Earth - the belief you can make money from the size of other people's wallets.

This was the religion of the dwarves, that from another's pocket your life shall be paid. Some say that the road to Hades is paved with Shamway products, others suggest that the lords of Chaos secretly invented the religion of MLM to break down the order of society. And you have to admit, calling a business opportunity a religion seems a bit rich, which paradoxically was the entire reason for making it a religion, because with the tax-free status when you got rich, you kept it.

Which is exactly the sort of greed the Lords of Chaos had counted on. It seemed like an innocent looking profit margin the person was after, but the real purpose was to set father against son, mother against daughter, and relative against relative - for what does MLM do best? It destroys all bonds of trust. You only know how evil it is when you go to your cousin with a business opportunity and he attacks you with a pickaxe, screaming, "not bloody Shamway!" as he seeks to end your life.

What better way to sow the seeds of destruction into society? The way it works is insidious: When you are afraid to answer your phone for fear of another business opportunity, you start to close off and become insular. Soon, you disconnect from society altogether, and in silence you brood. Finally, as the hammer of doom falls, you open the inner door to the whispers of chaos, and madness descends.

Proof of this was the recent elevation of the Trumpetus Orange, now Rex, as the King of New Rome. However, none of this affected dwarven society, because even at the best of times, they never trusted each other and their entire world was based on greed and selfishness - which is possibly why they were so successful in Shamway.

The dwarves were not fools. The main purpose for having a relative was to have someone to blame for the things you stole, which meant MLM was good for the family because with Shamway you could effectively steal and be entirely blameless. Apart from the tax-free status of a business being a religion being dubious, you may also ask about the ethics of taking money off poor innocents, but I say relax. It was known that if a common man were to be given large amounts of money, or even a weekly wage sufficient to cover expenses, soon after shall come a dwarf to get it off him. This is a constant of the Universe with a clear argument based on science and Einsteinium's famous equation of Energy (E) equaling Matter (M) times the Speed of Light (C) Squared.

This is well known to all, but what few grasp is the ultimate power of the speed of dark. Sure, light has a velocity, but as soon as you have light BOOM, shadow appears. Therefore the Speed of Dark is ALSO a constant, one that is considerably faster than the speed of Light. As money ($) is the main form of energy that the dwarves worship, and because it matters (M) so much to them, and as the Speed of Dark (SD) is infinite, this means it is infinitely more important to look after money, which means you get everything that matters. So: $M + SD = \$$.

If this is unclear to you, the equation has been constrained to the simple proverb, Money Matters.

This is, of course, the cause of the rise of the Impressionists, because some fool in Paris who could not read or write English properly, wrote it as Monet Matters, thus making art fashionable, therefore profitable, and so it became the latest product brought into the Shamway catalog.

All of the above is important, for just as the last of the exhausted riders wheeled into the town of the Fox Hat makers, the werewolves, who had been running hard, looking for an easy meal of bicyclists, rushed headlong into the very confusing situation of fox hats. The dwarves were there, all with Fox Hats in hand, selling them as the latest addition to the Shamway range. The whole damn town was full of Fox Hats! They sniffed, and it was clear these odd people must be relatives, yet they were also food. They needed to discuss what was up, so all the werewolves headed back out of town for a meeting, and in the meantime, they may as well have a party, because this is what they do.

A Confudled Rufus

I am well aware that as much as I wanted this story to be over, it was not. There were many loose ends to tie up, but I was happy to leave them like that because, quite honestly, don't you get a little tired of the happily ever after thing? Yet, as I was trying to sneak out the back door, I got pulled up by Rufus. "You!" he called out, apparently noticing for the first time the narrator of this tale, "What are YOU doing here?"

I confess to blushing, for narrators are not supposed to be part of the story, and are meant to float above it with wise observations and pithy wit. One supposes narrators live on a cloud and observe things, but this is incorrect - we are invariably up close and personal, but living in a slightly separate dimension, like the vampires, where there is a sort of one-way mirror effect - I can look in, but the players in the story cannot see me watching, unless they are Demi-gods or higher.

It was Meridius who spoke, "It's the narrator, sweetums. He has been with us since the start, telling our story. He is part of the reason we are famous."

Rufus just looked confudled, "But I thought WE were the reason we were famous!" he objected. "And if he has been with us the whole time, how come I never noticed?"

Meridius tut-tutted him, "Rufus, you have to be a Demi-God or higher to see narrators, you know, above the plot line and all that."

"But I AM a Demi-God! I even drove Zeus' chariot to prove it!" he objected.

Ofal then wandered up looking slightly less blank and a fraction more curious. "What, you mean you never saw our narrator before? He's been with us the whole time. I thought he was part of the crew."

Rufus looked suspiciously at Ofal, then back at Meridius, then at me (fairly accusingly I might add) before asking, "So you are saying OFAL is a Demi-God as well? I mean, honestly, this depreciates the value of Demi-Godery to a fairy HUGE degree, you have to admit!"

A which point Vulcan wandered over, "Thanks ever so much for looking after my boy, Meridius. I am sorry if I caused trouble, but honestly, these Gods need to be taught a lesson."

Ofal looked very shy, "Hi Dad," he murmured."Since when you had Thor as an apprentice?"

Vulcan put his fingers to his lips, the ancient sign of 'shhh'. "He is working cheap as a spy for Odin. Using his OWN hammer to beat out swords, and doing a damn fine job, I might add."

At this point Orpheus stumps up, smiling as all seemed to have ended well, but with a question on his brow. "Ah, Vulcan old chap, that sword you made, which Hercules has, and which the dragon can't seem to distract him from - what it is?"

"A song sword, something right up your alley, Orpheus. If you swing it when asking a question it emits tones that cut between dimensions. So it opens you up to wherever you want to go, and can send people to wherever you want them sent."

The wisest of Humans nodded slowly, then asked a very simple question, but cleverly offered an explanation in front of it, because Vulcan, despite him making the sharpest of tools, was not so sharp himself. "Well, the reason I ask is that Hercules has it in his possession, and on his shoulder is the Ancient Dragon of Imagination. Together this would pretty much represent ultimate power. Do you think it is wise to leave those things with him?"

Vulcan laughs, a hearty laugh that shakes the ground, "Oh, no need to worry. The safest person in the world to have a Dragon of Imagination on their shoulder is Hercules. Why? Because he has absolutely no imagination whatsoever, so can't wish for anything good or bad. And the sword, well, it's a nice toy and he may as well keep it because no one pays for their stuff anyway."

"But," Orpheus protested, "that is possibly your greatest work! Better than Excalibur, and you are leaving it with, forgive me for saying, possibly the most stupid Demi-God to have ever existed?"

Vulcan shrugged, "Well, on the plus side, being as he is Hercules there is zero risk of anyone stealing it off him and using it for evil. I mean, let's face it, that is what I was going to do - open the door between order and chaos and let in the Lords of Chaos. Then, as the saying of the games went, 'Let 'em at it!' - I was reasonably confident that this would have pretty much leveled the Gods and Demons, and everything in between. Honestly though, would it have been SUCH a bad thing? The Earth would do much better without the lot of them..."

Vulcan's thoughts trailed off as Meridius crossed her arms again and gave him a stern look. "OK, I promise to leave well enough alone. We will let Hercules keep the sword and the little dragon, though she IS very cute. I want to keep Myrtle, however!"

At which point a delighted dragon wobbled over with soft, luminescent eyes and snuggled up to the blacksmith. He rubbed her

behind the ears, telling her how lovely she was, and she PURRED.
"Awww," Vulcan melted, "sooo cute, and SO pretty!"

Myrtle fluffed her feathers and went positively love-struck. And here
is the thing, people imagine that because Dragons jealously guard hordes
of gold, that gold is what they love. Gold will DO, because it warms the
butt, but what Dragons love most is PURPOSE. You see, for the very
first time in her life, Myrtle felt she had a true and worthwhile purpose.

What could be a better match? She with her dragon breath, and
Vulcan with his big brawny arms, and sexy beard, and lovely teeth - I
mean - his ability to beat metal into things. The little dragon sighed - She
couldn't deny it any longer. What had happened was Myrtle fell in love!
She was SO much in love she had even hatched an egg for the beautiful
Mr. Vulcan. She had presumed it would be unrequited, but when Vulcan
said he wanted HER, well - she became putty in his hands.

The others just stopped as the little dragon purred, rubbed her head
against his leg, and looked up at her man with soft, glistening eyes of
cuteness. And gruff, rude, crude Vulcan became Mr. Nice and even
threw a stick for her to fetch, not understanding why she looked at it,
then at him, then at the stick, before sending a puff that turned it to ash.

Vulcan cheered and threw another one, and she happily purred and
turned it to toast. And they may have happily played like this for hours,
only a grey cloud appeared as a set of stairs opened in the ground, and
the killjoy joined the party. Hades stomped up from the underworld,
demanding why all the Gods were not dead and in his care - and THEN
he sees Meridius, Merlin, Orpheus, the Ogoglio, and some other nere-do-
wells, all smiling.

But far worse, there was Hercules with the Gateway Sword AND the
Dragon of Imagination, the two things Vulcan was supposed to be using
the destroy the world. THEN he sees Vulcan, happy and laughing and
playing with a feathered dragon, it was all too much. Hades demanded,
"Where are my people!"

Which struck a curious note with Hercules, because if you recall from
Rome Tree, when he only knew himself as Brutus Maximus, Hercules
had conquered the hearts and minds of the werewolves and they had
made him the clan chief. "Yes," said Hercules to himself, scratching his
head with his sword, "Where ARE my people?"

At which point, his Dragon of Imagination lit up and went "Omph" in
his direction, which made Heracles laugh, thinking it was a great game,
and he replied with a "Whoomph!" So his Dragon went "Omph" again,
excitedly, and he replied with a "Whoomph!"

Though it seemed entirely innocent fun, this action caused a rift between the worlds to form. There was a rolling of thunder, a flashing of lightning, and a portal appeared in the sky above them. Then, the most extraordinary thing: A chicken emerged, fully formed from out of the ether, going, "Bok bok bok".

Orpheus cried out in delight, "Now we FINALLY know which came first!" he exclaimed. And he pulled out his notebook and made an entry, "We thought Chicken Eggs came from dragons farts - how wrong could we have been? It must therefore be cats," he writes in careful copperplate.

You see good people, when holding the Gateway Sword and asking a question such as this, then going "Oomph" and "Whoomph", you are drawing a portal. In this case, it was in response to the question of where these people of Hercules might be. As we know, these are the Werewolves, who were presently in a small valley outside the town where the riders of the Tour de Gaul had stopped. They were wondering what to do - the dwarves were putting up very convincing arguments about joining Shamway, which got them scratching their heads (not from fleas) because while it meant they could make a lot of money, therefore party harder, it ALSO meant they could not eat their customers, as this would ruin their downstream.

Then the portal opens and they see their clan chief, Hercules, waving to them with a sword, and beyond that, there was good old Hades, their last landlord who they never paid any rent to. But even better, past him the doorway to the Underworld was open. Fantastic, two birds with one stone - They can get back home AND they will have an income! The werewolves all leaped up and ran through the portal, grabbing Hades, dragging him with them, saying, "Have WE got a deal for YOU!"

Brutus Maximus just shrugged his shoulders and followed the werewolves down to where Uncle Hades lived. "There is only one certain thing in all the universe," he said to the invisible dragon that now sat happily on his shoulder, "where there are fun-loving fellows like that, a good party is sure to follow. They are a little hairy, mind, but they have excellent teeth."

Merlin just scratched his head, not entirely sure what had happened, but as it seemed to work out fine he supposed that it was, except he didn't have anything for his efforts. "Ah, you people are not concerned that while he has that dragon and that sword every question Hercules asks, or is even ASKED, will get answered? Doorways to everywhere will just open up anywhere in the multiverse to provide the solution!" he looked questioningly at the crew before him.

You see, the WHOLE reason Merlin was in this story was because he was the one who made Excalibur famous. As that was the last great God Sword that Vulcan made, Merlin figured (rightly) that when the ancient blacksmith asked for a dragon, and that he now possessed the Omphalos, it meant he was about to make another one. If he could get his hands on this new one he might be able to reclaim a bit of past glory. However, given that he let the last sword get tossed into a lake, never to be seen again, I feel you will agree with me that perhaps he didn't deserve another chance.

Even so, it was an odd turnout. Orpheus laughed at the absurdity, "It is true, this is a somewhat curious result, but as Hercules has gone down to the underworld with only werewolves for friends, it is a fairly safe bet that the only question THEY will be asking is where the next party is."

The Ogoglio nods, "And this solves the problem of the Werewolves. More to the point, I say that is probably the most fun place right now!" And so he, too, ran down the still existing stairs to the underworld. "Wait up Hercules!" he called out.

Rufus was almost morose, "Then I suppose it's a happy ever after for everyone." He was now feeling so very unimportant, even OFAL was a Demi-God! When he first found out he was the brother of Hercules, for a brief moment he felt truly superior to someone. Now he just felt horribly ordinary.

Which was when Meridius planted a big, red lipstick kiss on his cheek. "Thank you SO much for not being Ogoglio, darling," she said. (which brightened him up tremendously) "Now, to you pair!" The Oracle looked directly at the Trumpetus Rex and Rupus Murdochius.

"Hey, I am down a dragon!" complained the Trumpetus.

"And I am missing an end-of-world story I promised the readers!" complained Rupus Murdochius.

"Hmmmm," said Meridius in a very severe tone.

The Trumpetus looked at his toes, "Well, technically yes, you don't own a dragon, you just bribe it to sit on your gold, true. But I have gone to a lot of trouble for nothing ..."

Murdochius sighed, "Yes well, I suppose it is better the world hasn't ended, and I guess I can write up the *'Dragon meets blacksmith and falls in love'* bit." But what he is thinking of writing up is, "Invisible Dragon goes off with brutal murderer, plotting in the underworld to destroy all of mankind." He would have to make it tighter for a headline - maybe, "Good Guy Goes Bad!" with the subtitle of Hercules teaming up with an evil Dragon - that would work.

Meridius just sighs and looks over to Merlin with a raised eyebrow. The magician rolled his eyes, feeling very sorry that he had such a small bit part in this entire drama. Finally, he relented. "Oh alright," he says. And with a wave of his wand, he and the pair he had brought to Mount Vesuvius vanished, presumably back to New Rome.

For the next few years, the Trumpetus Rex could only speak of one thing, "You know, my Dragon was stolen from me!" But other than that, things pretty much went back to normal.

And so we come to the end of our tale. The world has survived, Rome still rules, and life carries on. The only thing I feel that I need to advise you all of is this - be very careful about who you invite to your next party, for you MAY end up meeting a few too many party animals.

Final Awards

It was some weeks later that Eruptus Non-Funnius appeared at the closing ceremony of the Tour De Gaul. Everyone wore their best togas and smiled at each other as if they cared, but the only thing on anyone's mind was, "Do I get an award?"

There were a range of awards, from, "Fastest 100 Meter" to "Longest Climb" to "Ducked Most Rocks" and as they were handed out, each of the riders started with something akin to, "I want to thank (Insert their regions specific God) for giving me the courage to try when I wanted to give up" etc. Those with advertizing contracts would also thank the ball bearing manufacturer, or whoever sponsored them, and everyone thanked their mother, and wished she were here to see this.

The fact that she was sitting at home, knitting, and not watching the ceremony because she had always said her boy or girl should have gotten a proper job, and not just pedaled about, was never mentioned.

But the thing about sports awards, no one ever says, "I am unworthy of this accolade." It is not like an award for theatre, where you can bribe the judges to say your Shakespeare a little better than the next persons - No, you had to actually win an event. Of course, you may well have been doped to the eyeballs and spiked the competitors drinks in order to do it, but there is nothing subjective about who crossed the line first.

Yet, if you think about it, no one at any award ceremony ever (even such stupid ones as, "Best Polished Pan" in the Chef's awards) declared they are unworthy of it, despite the fact they cheated, bribed, slept with, and cajoled the judges to tick them off.

There were some questions about the Scots winning the "Best playing of bagpipes when crossing the Pyrenees" award but not because there was no one else in the race. (at least no one left alive by the end, that is) The problem with this award was that the question about what was under the kilt was answered in no uncertain terms. Hamish McTaggart, the team manager, was at pains to explain to the press that his lads could not keep their kilts down as they were having a hard enough time playing the pipes one handed as it was.

THAT comment was blown all out of proportion, and "Playing the Pipes One Handed" became the favorite T-Shirt of the games.

However, no one mentioned the elephant in the room, the gossip about Zeus and Loki. No one, that is, until Meridius, who had been asked to make the closing comments.

Typically, she thanked everyone, especially the losers, because without them there could have been no winners. This eased the tension in the room and many of the losers put down the knives they were about to put into the back of the winners, to listen to what she had to say.

The Oracle then tapped the microphone, and went, "Hmmmm." Most assumed she was reading their thoughts, but in this instance, she was wondering how to best say what needed to be said. She called up her boys, as she affectionately thought of them, and so Ofal and Rufus joined her, To their surprise, she put her arms around both of them as they came up on either side.

"It is a good thing to have a friend," she stated. Rufus and Ofal blushed, but she paid it no attention. "My life as the Oracle had been a very lonely thing and because of this I ran away, which was when I discovered friends. With these good friends I found a whole new world out there, one where I could make a difference.

"We traveled to New Rome and to Canadia, we were chased by authorities, augurs, and angry crowds, but we stood together, as friends. We met many wonderful people and had the most brilliant fun, and I am here to tell you that THIS is what matters. Life isn't about a popularity contest or a competition, it is about finding the right friends and enjoying their company. It isn't about being rich, or worshipped, or being thought highly of by others, it is about being loved by those you love. In the end, this is the only thing that really matters.

"It doesn't matter what others think. It doesn't matter what they say. The only thing that matters is that you have a friend who loves you, for in this lonely world, in this harsh place, they are your resource and your succor. What happens when you have no money? It doesn't matter because you know your friends will feed you. And if you don't have a place to stay? A good friend will give you his donkey cart to sleep in. Together you will make the world a better place, and that is what really counts. Thank you."

There is rapturous applause as Eruptus non Funnius, that legendary band of fellows, waves to the crowd and exits stage left.

Rufus has a tear in his eye, not really knowing what to say, but feeling all sorts of Ogoglio, yet humble at the same time. Ofal was the one who spoke, but the roaring applause drowned out whatever he had to say, so we will never know what it was.

Vulcan had been tuning in with Myrtle, who had convinced him in her winsome, featherly dragon way to pay some attention to what happened in the world. When he looked a little confused at the notion of a friend, she snuggled in, to remind him what it was. (She had great wisdom in this, for no one wants to end the world when they have a good friend, you see - but she was never rude enough to point this out.)

It was Zeus who really blubbed, sitting there with Loki on their private little mountain top. In many ways, it was the perfect arrangement, Loki would transform himself into one beautiful woman after another, thus satisfying the need Zeus had to roam, and he never ever turned back to a man while they were making love, thus easing his guilt over being gay.

The big guy had finally realized with the speech by his favorite Oracle just what he could tell Hera. It was so easy, Loki was his good friend that he liked to hang out with. And, as she would never believe he could possibly be gay, all his problems were solved!

Hera, of course, was not fooled, and knew what he was up to with the God of Tricks - but as long as she wasn't embarrassed by another woman in his life, she really didn't mind. In all, the perfect ending.

Well, for almost everyone. Hades, of course, went around moaning, and covering his ears from the deafening sounds of werewolves howling as they had one party after another. But he was always miserable so no one really noticed, or cared.

Because, no one likes a killjoy, do they?

End Notes

It took some time, but finally, Myrtle convinced Vulcan to invest in a recycling yard, where he discovered the delight of taking large amounts of money from foolish humans for things he could never have imagined were worth a bean.

All those years complaining about how the Gods never paid for anything, and one little dragon shows him the way to build up a gold horde. He cheered up enormously after that, which was good for the planet as we had a lot less by way of volcanic explosions.

This only proved how wise Myrtle the love-struck dragon was, for love can fade, but commerce and recycling will last forever. Or at least until the insurance claim.

MAJOR FIRE AT DRAGON RECYCLING

tinyurl.com/mw6t3bx2

Author Notes

A huge shout out to Jim Green for giving me the story line of this third book in the Rome series. The Jolly Green Giant is as good a friend as anyone could find, and without him this book would have stayed in the puzzlement stage of inception.

Also, my thanks to my son, EJ for his excellent observations on the nature of bookmakers. I felt something was missing, and he provided the last piece of the jigsaw.

Also, thanks to Miss Hamilton, to whom I mercilessly and cruelly expressed thoughts and notions that ended up in this book. If her razor wit and rending sarcasm could not trim the extraneous edges off an idea, nothing would.

However, a small warning, you may be tempted to take some of the notions in this book seriously. This would be a grave mistake, or at least a rabbit hole experience, one you may never return from. Just do not do it! Silliness is its own reward and like reading "Three Men in a Boat" by Jerome K Jerome, deep literary insights are very much best left to one side.

Any resemblance between persons living or dead is very unlikely to be coincidental, and names have been changed to protect the guilty.

Let your boat of life be light, packed with only what you need - a homely home and simple pleasures, one or two friends, worth the name, someone to love and someone to love you, a cat, a dog, and a pipe or two, enough to eat and enough to wear, and a little more than enough to drink; for thirst is a dangerous thing.
Jerome K. Jerome

ROME TOO and TREE

If you liked ROME TOR, you will love the rest of the books in the series.

Crazy madness disguised as mere frippery underscores out present state of affairs in a way you will find stupidly funny yet horribly true. The Rome series is a satire on the whole of Western Culture. Written in the tradition of Jerome K Jerome and his famous Victorian novel "Three men in a Boat", the book that instigated absurdist British humor and gave rise to such acts as the Good Show and the Monty Python tradition.

You will laugh, you will cry. Well, not really, the books are far too silly to cry over. Take a break from reality and immerse yourself in a bit of nonsense that has been favorably compared to Terry Pratchett, Douglas Adams, and Jasper Fforde.

Publisher: Ladder to the Moon Productions
Email: qrcaustralia@gmail.com
Web: laddertothemoon.com.au

Book
of
Yeshua

Ecaltaw Leachim

The Voice for Truth in a World of Lies

A lyric and simply beautiful book. You walk in the footsteps of
Yeshua, through the politics and intrigue of Ancient Judea, and into
the heart of his teaching, but through the eyes of the Essene faith.
This narrative offers a unique and deep insight into the true core of
what was to become Christianity.

Available on AMAZON

Hunters of the Mist

COPYRIGHT 2021 Ladder to the Moon Publications
Author: Ecallaw Leachim
ISBN: 978-0-6452723-0-7

Was this planet even Earth? Some sort of cataclysm has descended and the sun itself no longer shines upon the land. The crew of the Canter return after an extended away time to find a suffocating mist covers most of the land, a mist that houses creatures of horror who seek to dominate all that come near them.

Small pockets of humanity remain, but it is like the stone age. Jack Blake undertakes an arduous program, one that runs for decades, slowly educating the primitive people to perform the most basic tasks of civilization. And through it all, the Gregorians, the witch hunters track into the mist and free the land from control by the aliens that have taken residence in it.

Publisher: Ladder to the Moon Productions
Email: qrcaustralia@gmail.com
Web: laddertothemoon.com.au

Touchani Mandalas

Mandalas of Perception

Touchani is an ancient word that means more than seeing, more than perception - it is knowing a thing from the inside out. It is intimacy, clarity, and a sense of deep connection. In Sanskrit, the closest word is Vidya.

A Mandala is an object of contemplation, designed to focus the mind and bring in a connection to a higher spiritual force.

The purpose of the Touchani Mandalas is to open your consciousness to a new state. They will help transform ordinary minds into enlightened ones and assist with healing, as well as personal growth. They help bring about the state of spiritual freedom - Jivan Mukti.

The creator of the art is called "The Garji". Garji, in Sanskrit, means, "The roar of approaching thunder". It symbolizes the answer to the question, "What is the Sound of One Hand Clapping?" The word denotes an opening between the planes where the benevolence of the heavenly worlds flows into the physical existence. It is an opening (Mudra) that precedes and prepares for the State of Grace.

Just observing these Mandalas for ten minutes a day will bring about a shift in consciousness and answers to your deepest questions.

Available on Amazon

ROME TOR

COPYRIGHT 2022 Ladder to the Moon

ISBN: 978-0-6452723-2-1
Copyright 2022 Ladder to the Moon
Publisher: Ladder to the Moon Productions
Email: qrcaustralia@gmail.com
Web: laddertothemoon.com.au

About the Author

Ecallaw Leachim is considered by many to be
a polymath. He is accomplished in many
diverse fields, as a Master Musician, Master
Body Worker, Master Numerologist, Dice
Master, Recording Artist, Songwriter, and
Publisher. On top of all this he is also a prolific writer
with over twenty titles in print.

www.laddertothemoon.com.au

Aiming for the Stars is much easier if we stop off at
the Moon. We are then out of the atmosphere of our
past, and can see things more clearly. We are lighter,
can jump higher and further than ever before, and it
takes far less energy to start each journey.

The hard part is climbing that Ladder to the Moon.